John Creasey -

CW01499782

Born in Surrey, England in 19(
were nine children, John Creas
teller and international sensation. His more than 600 crime, mystery
and thriller titles have now sold 80 million copies in 25 languages.
These include many popular series such as *Gideon of Scotland Yard*,
The Toff, *Dr Palfrey* and *The Baron*.

Creasy wrote under many pseudonyms, explaining that booksellers
had complained he totally dominated the 'C' section in stores. They
included:

> *Gordon Ashe, M E Cooke, Norman Deane, Robert Caine Frazer,
> Patrick Gill, Michael Halliday, Charles Hogarth, Brian Hope, Colin
> Hughes, Kyle Hunt, Abel Mann, Peter Manton, J J Marric, Richard
> Martin, Rodney Mattheson, Anthony Morton* and *Jeremy York*.

Never one to sit still, Creasey had a strong social conscience, and
stood for Parliament several times, along with founding the One
Party Alliance which promoted the idea of government by a
coalition of the best minds from across the political spectrum.

He also founded the British Crime Writers' Association, which to
this day celebrates outstanding crime writing. The Mystery Writers
of America bestowed upon him the Edgar Award for best novel and
then in 1969 the ultimate Grand Master Award. John Creasey's
stories are as compelling today as ever.

THE TOFF SERIES

A Bundle for the Toff

A Doll for the Toff

A Knife for the Toff

A Mask for the Toff

A Rocket for the Toff

A Score for the Toff

Accuse the Toff

Break the Toff

Call the Toff

Double for the Toff

Feathers for the Toff

Follow the Toff

Fool the Toff

Hammer the Toff

Here Comes the Toff

Hunt the Toff

Introducing the Toff

Kill the Toff

Leave It to the Toff

Kiss the Toff

Model for the Toff

Poison for the Toff

Salute the Toff

Stars for the Toff

Terror for the Toff

The Kidnapped Child

The Toff among the Millions

The Toff and Old Harry

The Toff and the Crooked Copper

The Toff and the Deadly Parson

The Toff and the Deep Blue Sea

The Toff and the Fallen Angels

The Toff and the Golden Boy

The Toff and the Great Illusion

The Toff and the Lady

The Toff and the Runaway Bride

The Toff and the Sleepy Cowboy

The Toff and the Spider

The Toff and the Stolen Tresses

The Toff and the Toughs

The Toff and the Terrified Taxman

The Toff and the Trip-Trip-Triplets

The Toff at Butlins

The Toff at the Fair

The Toff Breaks In

The Toff Goes On

The Toff Goes to Market

The Toff in New York

The Toff in Town

The Toff in Wax

The Toff Is Back

The Toff on Board

The Toff on Fire

The Toff Proceeds

The Toff Steps Out

The Toff Takes Shares

Vote for the Toff

Murder Out of the Past (short stories)

The Toff on the Trail (short stories)

Score for The Toff

John Creasey

HOUSE OF
STRATUS

This edition published in 2012 by House of Stratus, an imprint of Stratus Books Ltd., Lisandra House, Fore Street, Looe, Cornwall, PL13 1AD, U.K. www.houseofstratus.com

Typeset by House of Stratus.

A catalogue record for this book is available from the British Library and the Library of Congress.

ISBN 07551-3631-4
EAN 978-07551-3631-5

Acknowledgments

I am most grateful to Mr. Brian Castor, of the Surrey County Cricket Club, to the Oval authorities generally, and in fact to the English team – all of whom helped me so much, some wittingly, some unwittingly, in the preparation of this book.

I would like specially to mention two Ovalites, Mr. J. Gillingwater and Mr. G. Ives, who not only found me an orange box on which to stand and see over the heads of the crowd, but – quite spontaneously – presented me with several of the remarks which I have put into the mouth of the character Ebbutt.

The writing of the book gave me a lot of fun, for from my earliest days, I have watched Surrey play at the Oval. Although cricketers are no longer gods, to me they remain the heroes of the greatest of games.

John Creasey

Author's Licence

There are no rooms at the Oval to which ladies can be admitted, but for my meeting between Bella Daventry and the Toff, one was necessary. So I cheerfully called upon author's licence. They should first have met in the Ladies Pavilion, too, but I couldn't bear to have Rollison anywhere but among his fellow members.

J.C.

Chapter One

Mr. Rollison Says No

"No," said Richard Rollison, absently. "Impossible. Tell him how sorry I am."

He smiled.

He could not have smiled more warmly or more attractively had the man to whom he was saying "no" been in the room instead of at the other end of a telephone wire. True, the intermediary was present, in Jolly, who served Rollison in many capacities; but the casual if courteous negative was not meant for Jolly.

Jolly did nothing to pass the refusal on, but hugged the mouthpiece to his unmanly bosom, and regarded Rollison with great, brown, soulful eyes. Rollison sat at a large desk in a comfortable chair; reading.

It was an English summer day, which the sun and the rain, the clouds and the mists had not betrayed. Already, at half-past nine, it was pleasantly warm. In an hour it would be hot, in two very hot indeed by English standards, which are higher in heat than all except natives realise. And in two hours' time the English, with the Welsh, the Scottish, the Cornish and some Irish, not to mention a noble few from the Southern Hemisphere, would be forgetful of world problems, film stars' tantrums, Dior and Hartnell, divorce, murders, economic plights, political upheavals – all those and other things. Radio, television, the naked eye and all the known senses of man would be tuned to a green field and flannelled fools. Men who were men, and women who were worthy of them, would be held in a mystic thrall of battle; the battle for the Ashes.

The battlefield was London's Oval, across London's broad river from here. Already Rollison, so casual yet emphatic about his "no", was wondering whether he should leave this flat in Mayfair at half-past ten or a quarter to eleven; nothing in this world that he could prevent would stop him from seeing the first ball bowled in mortal combat.

So preoccupied was he, while reading typescript pages and thinking about cricket, that he did not realise that Jolly still hugged the telephone. Jolly's mouth worked. Jolly was obviously going to speak, but found the appropriate words difficult to utter.

Explosively: "Sir!" he burst out.

Rollison started, and looked up.

"Eh?"

"Sir, I—"

"I didn't hear the thing ring," said Rollison, "who is it this time?"

"It didn't ring," Jolly declared, in a hoarse voice. "It—"

"Now that is what I call real brilliance," declared Rollison, and beamed up at his man with great pride and affection. "You've tuned yourself in so well that when the infernal machine is about to ring, wham! off comes the receiver. The Post Office ought to know about your system; when the game's over remind me to send a report."

He beamed again; then looked distastefully at the typescript; then glanced at his watch.

"Sir," said Jolly, thinly, hopelessly, "this is the original call. The gentleman is still holding on. I am hoping that you will change your mind."

Rollison stared blankly. "What about?"

"That you will see Mr. McGinn, sir."

"Today?"

"Yes, sir. If you—"

"My dear chap," remonstrated Rollison, leaning back, "I've been overworking you. Don't blame yourself, the fault is mine. Coo a gentle no, then ring off and let me get you an aspirin. And go to bed.

I won't be back until the evening, and I can dine out anyhow. We mustn't let anything go wrong with you, you know."

Jolly, his skin usually a pale brown, his face lined, and with baggy jowl which suggested – wrongly – that he had slimmed from a vast weight to his present hundred and thirty-eight pounds, became positively ashen.

"I'm sorry, sir. I think you should see Mr. McGinn. The case may well be extremely remunerative. He mentioned a retainer of two hundred and fifty pounds, and made it clear—"

"But Jolly, you know what the day is!" Rollison almost squeaked. "Saturday, August the Fifteenth, in this year of Grace. I'm going to the Oval."

"You could see Mr. McGinn first, sir."

"What a persuasive gentleman he must be. Let me talk to him," said Rollison mildly, and stretched out his hand for the telephone. "Being an American, he wouldn't understand the sanctity of the day, of course. I might even be persuaded to see him tomorrow, as there's no play, but it had much better wait until the end of next week."

Jolly held tightly on to the telephone.

"He is a valuable client, sir."

"You mean, he could be. Gimme." Rollison stood up and flicked his arm; and as if by magic, the telephone sprang out of Jolly's hand and into his. He smiled again, not at Jolly but at the imagined picture of the unknown Mr. McGinn, whom he knew was staying at a large, luxurious hotel, also in Mayfair. "Mr. McGinn," boomed Rollison, in a controlled voice which would sound most impressive at the other end of the telephone, "this is Richard Rollison. I am extremely sorry that—"

"That Rollison in person?" a man boomed back.

The voice was as rich as the richest American voice can be. It had that strange, unmistakable cadence which the English either dote on or hate. It was not over-loud, but it reverberated in a controlled kind of way. As a Roland for Rollison's Oliver no voice could have been more suitable.

Rollison, to offset it, became crisp.

"Yes. I'm sorry that—"

"Let me tell you at once, Mr. Rollison, how proud I am to be speaking to the greatest private eye in Europe," boomed Mr. McGinn. "I've heard so much about you, but didn't think I'd ever have the great pleasure of hearing you at the other end of the telephone. You encourage me to great hope, Mr. Rollison, indeed you do. If you—"

"Mr. McGinn, I—"

"—will do me the honour of having lunch with me today, I will know I'm one of the really favoured few, Mr. Rollison." McGinn was as remorseless as a steam-roller or Senator McCarthy. "And I can explain my problem, also. I can't think of any other man so likely to solve it for me, and I have told your secretary that when I get service I *pay* for service. The only thing I ask for is the best."

"You're very good," said Rollison, almost humbly. "But I'm afraid it's impossible. I am engaged for luncheon today."

"You *are?*"

"Inescapably engaged."

"Well, that's too bad," reverberated Mr. McGinn, sounding in no way disappointed and certainly not discouraged. "If you knew as much I can tell you, Mr. Rollison, I believe you would escape from that engagement all the same, but I don't wish to interfere with your arrangements, sir. Not at all. So if you will be here at my hotel at twelve noon, for cocktails, I could tell you enough to—"

"It's too bad," Rollison slipped in swiftly, glancing almost desperately at Jolly, "but I am engaged all day."

"*All* day?"

"Until after seven o'clock this evening. But I have no free time this week or next, except in the evenings. I'm sorry, Mr. McGinn, but—"

"You want me to tell you something, Mr. Rollison?" boomed McGinn. "All my life I've believed that when two men of intelligence have a good reason to get together, why, sir, they get together. Difficulties just don't mean a thing, and that's what I've been told about you, that difficulties don't mean a thing to you. Now, sir, it's five minutes of ten. If you could come and see me—"

"I'm really sorry," said Rollison, in the humility of real admiration, "but it can't be done. Er—write to me."

"What's that?"

"I suggested that you should write to me."

"My dear sir," breathed McGinn, with the vigour of a bucolic sailor, "I couldn't put anything about this on *paper*. No, sir, that's unthinkable. If you had any idea of what it's all about, you would say the same thing. Listen, Mr. Rollison, you just stay right there. I'll come and see you."

"No, really—"

"It's no trouble, no trouble at all," McGinn assured him grandly, "I'll be there in two shakes of a dogie's tail. Don't feel disturbed on my account. Just stay right there."

He rang off.

Rollison started to form the word "but", only to give up, exude a long, deep breath which misted the black telephone, and then put it down very gently on its stand.

All this time, Jolly had been staring at him, standing motionless near the desk. He looked as if Rollison's face or the sound booming from the receiver, had hypnotised him. He swallowed hard while Rollison looked at him and as Rollison took out a snow-white handkerchief and dabbed his forehead.

"You knew what he was like," he accused.

"He—ah—well—ah, I knew that he was persistent," Jolly agreed. "He was on the telephone earlier, when you were in your bath. He reached the Miramar very late last night, I understand. But it wasn't his persistence which influenced me, sir. Nothing is farther from my thoughts than taking any step which might make you miss the cricket, but—"

"I should think not!"

"But I'm quite sure that it's within your capacity, *well* within your capacity, to hold Mr. McGinn's interest during the ensuing week, and give your full attention to his case as soon as the game is over." In his own style, Jolly could be a steam-roller too. "He believes it is urgent, but I am reasonably sure that it cannot be so urgent as he makes out. Millionaires *are* inclined to think that they must have instant service, and everything is vital to them. And Mr. McGinn—"

"Did you say a millionaire?"

"A dollar millionaire many times over."

"How do you know?"

Jolly became bland. "I made some inquiries from the Press, sir, after he had first telephoned, an hour or so ago. Mr. McGinn is in steel. There is no doubt at all about his wealth. He is also a connoisseur and a collector of precious stones. I imagine—"

"Jolly," interrupted Rollison, in an inflexible voice, "I don't care whether he's a billionaire in steel, coal, shipping, Wall Street or Coca-Cola. I am not interested in his hobby or his grand passions. Before I talked to him I knew it was a mistake to weaken. Now that I've heard him I know it would be fatal to have anything at all to do with him. I was never good with human steam-rollers. You shall deal with him, and tell him how sorry we are."

Jolly, who might have made a fortune on television, looked positively hurt.

"You mean that you won't stay, sir."

"Precisely that," said Rollison. He looked into the man's face, saw distress there, and inwardly relented. When Jolly believed in a thing, he fought for it; and Jolly knew that a wealthy client was needed just now, for "the greatest private eye in Europe" had lived through a lean summer; his bank balance was precariously low. Now Jolly looked not so much disappointed as hurt; as a dog might look after an undeserved blow.

"Very well, sir," Jolly said, and turned away.

"If he's a minute after ten forty-five, I shall be gone."

Jolly spun round.

"But you *will* wait until then?"

Rollison grinned. "Why don't you kick me sometimes, Jolly?"

"Do you know, sir," said Jolly, "I am not a great believer in presentiments, but I have a conviction that you will be wise to accept Mr. McGinn's commission. I don't think that a man of his wealth and reputation would be so insistent if it weren't a matter of real importance. It may well be an investigation that you will enjoy. I should say that the motif is almost certainly precious stones. Will you excuse me, sir—I have not yet started on your bedroom."

"Start on," murmured Rollison.

He glanced down at the typescript, which was of a leading counsel's case for the defence of a very bad man who, thanks to great pleading, had escaped proper punishment. But Rollison was not really interested in it. As the door closed, he looked up at the door and the spot where Jolly had been.

He smiled—

He was a remarkably handsome man, and his grey eyes were fine and, just then, crinkled at the corners with a kind of affectionate amusement. He did not think much about the American McGinn, but a great deal about Jolly, who had been at some pains to find out what there was to know about the American. Jolly's concern was solely for his, Rollison's, bank balance.

It was then five minutes after ten.

Rollison read the brilliantly clever arguments which had helped the rogue to escape, admiring learned counsel's methods but seeing loopholes which, in future, would be firmly blocked.

At half-past ten Jolly came in with coffee on a silver tray.

"What hotel do you say McGinn's at?" asked Rollison.

"The Miramar, sir."

"If he'd left at once, he ought to be here."

"I feel sure he won't be long, sir."

"We can talk on the way," declared Rollison.

He drank coffee.

At a quarter to eleven he was at the window looking into the street for the American; and he was sure that Jolly was looking out of a bedroom window, too. He glanced at his watch, then at a clock on his trophy wall, a remarkable wall which he often took for granted. The minutes ticked by until it was eleven o'clock.

A sorely disappointed Jolly appeared at the door.

"I don't think it advisable to telephone the Miramar, sir, do you?"

"Not now," said Rollison, in a truly sympathetic tone. "Cheer up, man. It can't be as urgent as Mr. McGinn said, your philosophy on millionaires rang a bell. Just in case he turns up, give him this card." He took out a visiting-card and scribbled a note to that High Priest of the Week, the Secretary of Surrey County Cricket Club. "That'll get him into the ground, if the gates are closed, and officials will send word to me."

"You're very good, sir."

"Think nothing of it."

"I wish—" began Jolly, and stopped, forced a smile, and said: "I hope that you have a good day, sir, and that Mr. Hutton wins the toss."

"Mr. Hutton," declared Rollison, "will, most assuredly do his best. What did you wish?"

"It really doesn't matter, sir."

"Then I'll guess. You were wishing that this had happened on any day but this, because I'd be on my way to the Miramar instead of the Oval, to find out whether Mr. Millionaire McGinn left to come here. I'm not sure. You go, Jolly. Check, find him, find out why he didn't turn up and what he wants. Never let it be said," continued Rollison, "that you aren't the equal in astuteness of an American steel tycoon with a hobby of collecting jewels. I'll never believe it."

"I will do what I can, sir," Jolly promised.

It was four minutes past eleven when Rollison reached the street; five minutes past when he picked up a taxi. He kept an eye open for a man who might pass for an American, but saw no one. So he allowed the taxi-driver to work miracles in London's traffic.

He reached the Oval at twenty-six minutes past eleven, thrust through surging crowds, and such was his influence behind the scenes that he stepped out on to the front of the pavilion in time to see the massive might of Big Fella Bedser hurling the first ball of the Australian innings at a white-clad figure on that field of green.

He kept thinking of the absent Mr. McGinn.

After a while, he forgot Mr. McGinn.

The cricket was absorbing if not exciting, the mass of shirt-sleeved fans, all thirty thousand of them, watched each ball with bated breath. The fieldsmen and the batsmen moved with deceptive leisureliness. The television cameras, with their all-seeing eye, saw all that mattered, the radio announcers talked away to themselves in their little box, almost hermetically sealed, the news-reel cameras whirred, the sporting journalists made notes, grown men and small boys watched each trivial incident with a gravity which would have matched a battle for Mars. Twice the tension found release, once when Big Fella and once when Bailey wrapped Australian pads and claimed a kill – and won the umpire's signal, amid tumultuous applause.

Luncheon came and went, and Rollison thought fleetingly of Mr. McGinn.

Soon after lunch, Big Fella struck again with Evans leaping like a dancing dervish at the wicket. Then came new chum Trueman, like an avenging angel, to strike his savage blows.

Rollison, at the gangway end of a row of seats, was completely absorbed by young Master Trueman's slightly-turned-in toes as he bowled at venomous speed. Rollison was oblivious to all voices, until one very close behind him said: "Is that the one? Is that the Toff?"

She had a very dear, English voice, and her detachment from the game made Rollison and several others turn their heads. The moment they did so a roar went up. The ground, the stands, the pavilion, the brooding gasometers, the houses round the ground all resounded to a roar: *"He's out!"*

And Rollison, distracted by the young woman, had not seen the humbling of an Australian hero or the triumph of a youthful Yorkshireman.

He looked sourly upon the villainess, who regarded him as she might inspect an exhibit at a fair.

Chapter Two

The Villainess

The peak of excitement soon passed, and cramped fans sitting on the grass or on hard wooden seats stood up and moved about, with great relief, while the vanquished Australian came hurrying from the field, studying the turf and hiding his thoughts.

Most of the men who had turned to look at the girl, and so had missed that high-light, now looked away in deliberate disapproval. A few, the younger ones, continued to watch her. Two, very young, stared at Rollison as he stood up, and one of them breathed: "That's the *Toff.*"

A young man, bare-headed, looking amiable but rather distraught, smiled at Rollison.

"Hallo, sir. Sorry to interrupt. Miss—ah—Daventry says she has to see you on very urgent business. Miss Daventry, Mr. Rollison. Glad to have been of service. Must go. Goodbye."

He turned and hurried up the gangway towards the pavilion building.

The Australian about to bat was already half-way towards the wicket.

"We'd better find a quiet spot," said Rollison, who had made himself smile and do all the proper things, in spite of his ill-feeling.

He did not know Miss Daventry.

Had he met her in any other place, he would have had no regrets at all. But even a beautiful young woman with glorious golden hair and the most ravishing blue eyes should know better than to intrude upon such hallowed precincts, and it was not easy to be more than civil. Yet Rollison did not feel disposed to embarrass her by asking who she was and what she wanted within hearing of the ardent members, so he walked with her into the empty room – empty, that was, save for men jammed against the windows. The walls were hung with pictures of a hundred cricketers, past and present.

Miss Daventry said coldly: "I am sorry that I disturbed you." She did not look sorry, but rather as if she understood what was passing through his mind, and resented it.

"That's all right. How can I help?" He proffered cigarettes.

"No, thank you. I am not at all sure that you can help."

Rollison said: "Well, we can soon find out," and was nettled by her manner at the very moment when he was telling himself that her eyes did not depend on the sky for their brilliance. She wore a lemon-coloured linen dress with a bolero jacket, a kind of lavender-blue colour, and he had time now to realise that she had a sensational figure. And nice legs and ankles, too. Her arms were bare from just above the elbow, and she wore cotton gloves which matched her frock.

She took something out of a narrow pocket inside the exquisitely fitting jacket; a visiting-card. She handed it to him, and he glanced down. Immediately his mood changed; for this was his. She held it this way up deliberately, showing a pencilled drawing of a faceless man wearing a top-hat; a monocle, a cigarette in a holder and a bow tie completed the picture. It looked a kind of doodle sketch, but it served a double purpose. Many knew it as the Toff, for by that soubriquet Rollison was very widely known.

He turned the card over.

He had scrawled across his name and address – the Honourable Richard Rollison, 22g Gresham Terrace, London, W.1 – *only a few hours ago.*

"Dear Brian," he had written, "if you'll bring the bearer of this card to me, I'll be most grateful." And the then harassed secretary of the Surrey Club had done exactly that.

Mr. Millionaire McGinn, not a girl, should have brought it.

Still, Jolly had sent her; he would not have done so without feeling sure that it was wise or worthwhile.

"Do you know why Mr. McGinn didn't come to my flat?" asked Rollison, and then felt a flush of annoyance. Disappointment at having missed Trueman's blow, and preoccupation with other things, had concealed the obvious until now. Obviously, McGinn had sent an envoy rather than come himself. So he went on flatly. "I wanted to tell him quite clearly that I cannot accept any commission for at least a week." When the girl didn't answer, but looked at his almost disdainfully, he went on: "Will you be good enough to tell him that?"

"I would," she said, "if I could find him."

That jolted Rollison sharply, as it was meant to. Respect crept into his masculine admiration for Miss Daventry, but he didn't show it. Outside, there came a roar which made him turn his head; but it faded away; either a chance had been missed or a ball had beaten the bat. Rollison longed to be there, watching, for this game was in his blood; but he stood with the girl.

"Isn't he at his hotel?"

"No," she said. "I was to meet him there at noon today."

"And he stood you up?"

"Yes."

"As he did me," murmured Rollison. "Have you any idea why he wasn't there?"

"I hope I haven't." Miss Daventry still made no secret of her dislike of Rollison, and now he was mildly amused because she showed it so clearly. Her choice of word wasn't accidental, though: "I hope I haven't." Her eyes were quite calm and her manner was composed as she went on: "I am very anxious to find him, Mr. Rollison, but if he hasn't been here I don't see much point in staying. I am sorry that I interrupted your absorbing afternoon."

He grinned.

"Forgiven," he said brightly, "and if—"

A youth appeared, hurrying; he had the kind of look that a terrier might have if he knew exactly where to find a bone but had to pay respects to his master before unearthing it.

"Mr. Rollison wanted on the telephone," he said breathlessly, and his eyes turned towards a square of window through which he could see an infinitesimal patch of emerald green.

"Thanks. Where?"

"The secretary's office."

"I'll go at once," said Rollison, and turned again to the girl. "I'm sorry. If you can stay, let's have a cup of tea and see what we can work out. We've both been victimised by the same man, after all."

"You're very kind," she said stiffly, "but I will get in touch with you again, if necessary. Please don't let me keep you any longer." She inclined her head slightly, commanding him to go first; and, eyes laughing, he did so. But after he had slipped into the door leading to the secretary's room, he opened it an inch or two.

Miss Daventry walked past. Certainly her figure was sensational; she had hardly any waist at all. Her head was held high, and she had quite a chin. He thought that she was annoyed, either with him or cricket or men in general. As she had seen Jolly, Jolly would be able to tell him more about her.

Rollison went to the telephone.

It was Superintendent Grice, of New Scotland Yard; an old friend who would not choose this time and place for a call about personal things.

"Sorry to drag you away from the arena," he said, "I won't keep you long. I hope." That rider reminded Rollison of Miss Daventry.

"Kind heart," murmured Rollison, "say your brief say and begone, copper."

Grice chuckled. "How are you getting along with Mr. Connor McGinn, from Pittsburgh?" he asked. "Teaching him the finer points of the game?"

Rollison did not answer at once. At last his thoughts were torn completely from the field outside, and what was happening there. The magnetism of the emerald green and the nonchalant-looking men in white faded out as at the turn of a switch.

"I don't get it, Bill. He's not here."

"Do you mean to say he hasn't turned up?"

"This is the Oval, not Madison Square Gardens."

"He was all excited about going to see you at the British ball game," Grice said, and also sounded puzzled. "I thought he would have caught up with you. He'd telephoned Jolly, who told him where you were, and was about to rush off to collect the car. Didn't he—" It was Grice's turn to break off.

"He did not arrive here," Rollison said, firmly.

"Well, that's odd." The pause told Rollison that Grice was more than thoughtful; the tone suggested that he was worried. "Let me know if you hear from him, will you? He's in England with a fortune in precious stones; we had a request from New York to keep an eye on him for his own sake. Apparently he falls easily for con-men."

It was Rollison's turn to pause.

"Or he copies their methods," he said, almost sourly. "How did you know that he was on my tail?"

"I sent a man round to the Miramar," Grice explained. "My man saw Jolly, and discovered whom Jolly was after. So I talked to Jolly. I wanted a word with McGinn, too. You'll let me know if he shows up, won't you?"

"I will," promised Rollison. "You can have all of him, Bill."

This was obviously the moment when he could best tell the story of Miss Daventry and her card, but he let it pass. That was hardly his fault, for Grice said "goodbye", briskly, and rang off. Rollison put the receiver down, rubbed his chin, and felt no overpowering eagerness to return to his seat. He went slowly out of the office. The girl would be gone, and he wondered if Jolly knew where to find her. He also wondered what she had meant by: "I hope I haven't", when he had asked if she had any idea why McGinn hadn't arrived.

He went into the almost deserted entrance yard. Police and officials were still on duty at the gates. A small crowd was outside, as if hoping to get in. Just in sight, part of the crowd on the terraces was standing in sunlit stillness, watching each ball as if a life depended on it. Small boys called "Match cards", nice girls, youths and a few unshaven men carried blue boxes marked "Wall's", youths went round with strange syphons and contraptions marked "Pepsi-Cola".

The silence was broken by a heart-lifting, almost deafening roar from the crowd. Rollison spun round. Every hand in sight was being waved, hats were whirling, ice-cream cartons were spinning upwards, the crowd fell to an orgy of cheering and clapping. So Australia had lost another hero, and the Ovalites were telling some English bowler how they loved him.

A screech of brakes made Rollison swing round.

By the gates, a dozen people scattered, two terrified people were pressing against an iron gate as a small van bore down on them. One man was lying on the pavement – not on the road, the pavement – and the wheel of the van crushed his waist.

Around the great green field was elation.

At the gates was horror.

Chapter Three

Three-In-One

Rollison's faculty, given to few, of seeing and taking note of several things at once, switched automatically into action. The frightened group, two astounded policemen, several youths inside the gates who went running – all of those were on the perimeter of his mind.

Three things mattered.

First, the horrified face of the driver of the van. Second, the small car which was speeding away, its engine snorting as if the driver couldn't put trouble behind it fast enough. Third, the beauty of Miss Daventry as she stared from the open window of a taxi which started away from the road by the turnstile entrances.

Anyone seeing that accident, anyone only a few feet away from the wheel which crushed a man, would have been shocked. But few would show such horror as this girl did. It was naked and stark, and it froze the blue of her eyes and the red sweetness of her lips. One hand only was in sight, raised as high as her chin, the fingers crooked and stiff and the palm outwards, as if she wanted to fend off some menace which others could not see.

Then the police swung into action.

Three came hurrying to the help of the first two. Orders were issued quickly and calmly. A sergeant, tall, pale, lean, sweating in his blue serge and beneath his helmet, had an unexpectedly soothing voice. The girl's taxi-driver was told to stop where he was, the people were asked not to move, the driver of the van, still petrified, was not sworn at or cursed or called a killer; instead, he was helped.

"Just sit tight, we'll tell you what to do," the sergeant told him. "Sit tight."

"All—all—all right."

The sergeant joined two constables who were on their knees beside the crushed body. Could the man still be alive? Rollison glanced to see, to try to judge from the expressions of the police, but didn't desert the girl for long.

She was still staring. Her expression had changed slightly, becoming a land of frozen blankness. She was farther inside the taxi, now. The taxi-dxiver turned to say something to her, and her lips moved, slowly, stiffly. She looked like beauty carved out of ice.

People in the crowd began to talk.

"Is'he dead?"

"These damned drivers!"

"Look—look at the *blood.*"

"Let's get away from here, Charlie, I can't stand the sight of blood, never could."

"Didn't 'ave a chance, poor beggar."

These and a hundred other comments were like the waves of a murmuring sea. Rollison took no notice of them, but moved towards the iron gates. He could see over the heads of the police. The crowd had been quietly moved back, but not yet allowed to disperse, even if some wanted to; all were several yards from the body beneath the van.

The sergeant stood up.

"Better reverse a bit, will you?" He spoke to the van-driver, whose eyes were huge in his pale face, and whose lips were quivering and whose harsh voice shook.

"Is he—is he—"

"He's had it, I'm afraid."

"Oh, Gawd! I never meant—"

"Now take it easy," said the sergeant. "Just start the engine, put her into reverse, and go back a couple of yards. It's okay, we've got him clear of the wheel now."

"You—you sure he—"

"Do as you're told, will you?" The voice of authority took on a sharper note.

"Okay." The driver switched on his engine, and crashed his gears. Rollison saw the sweat on his forehead and his upper lip. He wasn't more than twenty-two or three, a dark-haired boy. "It wasn't my fault, it was that car what—"

"We'll sort it all out," said the voice of authority, soothing again. Then the sergeant raised it. "Now, who actually saw what was happening?" As the van moved back he looked about and then walked towards the taxi with Miss Daventry inside. Rollison felt sure that the sergeant knew that most of the people there had been looking into the Oval, not away from it. The taxi, about to move off, had been facing the scene of the smash, and so the driver might be a good witness.

Another policeman talked to officials inside the gates, men more likely to have been looking at the accident.

Rollison moved back towards the pavilion, went just inside, then came out again and walked briskly towards the gate. He frowned at the crowd as if surprised, and looked at a gate-keeper who wore a round badge printed with the letters S.C.C.C.; which made him a club official. The man knew him well.

"What's the trouble here, Jim?"

"Nasty do, Mr. Rollison, chap got run over. These accidents get worse an' worse, don't they? On the pavement, he was, too. Know what I'd do to these careless drivers? Put 'em inside, that's wot I'd do. Nothing short of murder, if you ask me."

"Dead, is he?" asked Rollison, avoiding argument. "Don't say the police are closing the gates."

"Oh, I 'spect you can leave," said the gate-keeper, "they're only looking for witnesses." He opened his gate and spoke to a constable who came up promptly. "Gent wants to go out, okay?"

"Did you see—?" began the constable.

"Only just come out of the pavilion." The gate-keeper did Rollison's lying for him, and Rollison was allowed to walk out.

The sergeant was still talking to the driver of Miss Daventry's taxi; the man had got out and was standing only as high as the sergeant's chin. The girl was sitting back in the cab, hardly visible. To avoid the crowd, Rollison crossed the road, walked a few yards, and then crossed again; when he reached the turnstile gates just behind the girl's taxi, the sergeant had put his head inside, to speak to her.

Rollison just heard him say: "Did you see it, Miss?"

Rollison heard no answer.

"All right, Miss, no need to detain you any longer," the sergeant said. "Sorry." He touched his forehead, and waved to the driver, who switched on his engine and began to move off.

Rollison got into the taxi behind.

"Follow the cab in front for a bit, will you?" he asked, in the most casual of voices, and as if by sleight of hand, placed a pound note within the driver's reach.

"Follow—"

"That cab in front. The one," added Rollison, with great deliberation, "in which the most beautiful girl in London is sitting."

The cabby, sleek and smooth and young, smothered a grin, pocketed his pound, and started off. Soon the cab was immediately behind the girl's. Rollison watched it, and thought of those three things in one: a disappearing Sunbeam Talbot, small, olive-green, powerful, with a fair-haired driver; the horrified face of the driver of the van as realisation of what he had done came over him; and the stark and naked horror on the face of a girl whose beauty had to be seen to be believed.

He had no other thoughts in his mind.

Then suddenly, thunderously, the comparative quiet of the day was broken by a roar from thirty thousand throats. It burst upon the afternoon's warmth with volcanic surge. And a strange thing happened. A hundred or so people, all in sight, all walking singly or in pairs along the pavement, stopped – or at the very least, missed a step. Every face was turned towards the high brick wall of the Oval. The drivers of passing cars and buses, vans and lorries, glanced that way too; and the cabby, like everyone else, instinctively slowed down.

Then, all the people in the streets, complete strangers to each other, forgot their traditional reputation for aloofness, and spoke as if to close friends. They beamed, grinned, chuckled, and walked along with jauntier step. The sleek, pale driver of Rollison's cab leaned his head back and, without turning round, said: "Wonder who we got now."

"It was a wicket we wanted, anyhow," said Rollison.

"S'right. Cor, wouldn't I like to beat the perishers this time! Think we've a chance?"

"I'm sure we've a chance."

"Hope you're right," said the taxi-driver. "Wouldn't I like to beat the perishers."

Then he and the walkers and the drivers and the passengers of other vehicles, resumed their normal pace and aspect. The Oval and the combat dropped behind. The Toff wrenched his thoughts from longing, and looked at the taxi he was following.

If he hadn't gone to look for the girl, he wouldn't have known about that dead man, and his conscience wouldn't have driven him away from the thing he most wanted to do in the world.

Miss Daventry got out of the taxi near Harrods, in the Brompton Road. It had stopped on the other side of the road from Harrods, where the pavement was very wide. Her long, elegant legs appeared first, and she emerged from the cab smoothly and swiftly; no mean achievement. She didn't look behind, but paid her cabby off. He saluted and moved away as Rollison was getting out of his cab. Rollison added ten shillings to the pound, and his driver was almost overcome by his gratitude.

"Any time," he concluded.

"You never know," murmured Rollison.

The girl was now walking slowly along the pavement. She looked as if she didn't quite know what to do or where to go. She was taller than he had realised before, her back was very straight, and she moved beautifully. A rear view would make most men quicken their step so as to see if the promise of loveliness was all it seemed to be.

Several men stared at her openly, several glanced furtively, three turned to look back.

Rollison reached the doorway of an antique shop. The girl approached a corner, then turned round slowly, to the embarrassment of a man who had just passed and was now staring back at her. Rollison felt quite sure that she did not notice the man.

She looked worried.

She walked in the other direction, glancing neither to the right nor the left. She was startlingly near perfection, and the blue of her eyes might have come fresh from the Bay of Naples and the translucent beauty of the Blue Grotto across the bay.

She did not glance towards Rollison.

In spite of her easy grace and the way she kept looking ahead of her, she showed many signs of nerves. Her right hand kept tightening on the handle of her bag; once or twice, the bag nearly slipped. The fingers of her left hand, held by her side, tightened, clenched, straightened, and clenched again. He could see that her cheeks were working, as if her jaws were clamping together.

She reached the end of the block, and turned yet again and walked back.

Several men now gave up all pretence and stood with their backs to the shop windows, simply to admire the girl; so the Toff was one of many.

A newsboy ambled past.

"Oval sensations, paper! Orstralian wickets fall fast, paper."

The girl walked up and down four times in all, then reached the corner on Rollison's right and, as if with sudden purpose, turned and moved swiftly along a wide street. He followed her. When he reached the corner, she was fifty yards along, walking quickly and apparently with great determination. It was as if she had fought and conquered fear, and was going to face a crisis.

Tall terrace houses, narrow, grey-faced, with long windows, porches, stone pillars, lace curtains and sign boards were on either side. Each sign board carried the same kind of message: *Apartments— Vacancies—Bed & Breakfast.* Here was a street once residential but now almost as diversely populated as a street of boarding-houses in Brighton or in Bournemouth.

A few houses had no apartments sign.

The girl turned into one of these, and walked up four stone steps. Her movements still had that grace which almost hurt, because it hinted at unattainable things.

She disappeared.

Rollison went to the open doorway. By the time he reached it, the girl was at the first landing. A wooden name board, standing just inside the narrow, gloomy hall, carried the names of people living in the flats; and none was named Daventry. Rollison made sure of that at a quick glance, then hurried up the stairs, making little sound.

A door opened on the second landing, and he saw it through the banisters.

Bright sunlight made shapely silhouettes of Miss Daventry's legs and ankles. She stood still, ankles close together.

A man's legs showed beyond them, grey-trousered, brown-shoed. Rollison kept very close to the wall and crept up the stairs, gradually seeing more; until he could see as high as Miss Daventry's waist.

"Bella!" a man exclaimed, with a strange, shrill force. "What the devil's the matter with you?"

"I must talk to you," the girl said. "It's urgent."

The legs and feet moved, then the door closed and the light vanished, leaving Rollison half-way up the stairs and most anxious to hear what the girl had to say. He went swiftly but made little sound, taking a knife out of his pocket as he moved.

He opened it to a skeleton-key blade.

Below him, a door opened and a deep, clear voice said:

"... two slips and a gully and deep third man. Hutton, of course, is at cover point, and—hallo, I think there's going to be a change of bowling. Hutton is talking to Trueman, oh, how well the Yorkshire lad has justified his selection in this crucial match! Hutton has bowled him very cleverly, using him in short spells. For the benefit of listeners who have just tuned in, the score is—"

The door closed, the sound became an indistinct murmur.

Rollison, almost astounded, found that he was standing and listening, with the skeleton key close to the keyhole but not inside it.

The girl might have finished the important thing she had to say.

"Damned fool," muttered Rollison, and slid the key into the lock and twisted and turned expertly, making hardly a sound.

The lock clicked back.

He took all this so much for granted that he turned the handle as readily as he would if he had used an ordinary key; but he pushed the door very carefully, and opened it only an inch.

A voice came from some way off, not in the room beyond.

"Why are you lying, Paul? I saw you there."

"You couldn't have done!" cried the man named Paul. "I wasn't anywhere near the Oval, it must have been someone like me."

Then there was silence.

Rollison pushed the door open wider, and stepped into a small hall. Leading off this were several doors, one of them open; and he could see the girl's back but nothing of the man.

He crept across the hall towards the door.

Chapter Four

Fair-Haired Paul

Rollison crossed the hall diagonally. The girl went out of sight. The couple hadn't spoken again; all Rollison could hear was heavy breathing of a man or woman who was almost panic-stricken.

Then the girl spoke. Her voice was low-pitched and emphatic; every word was uttered clearly and slowly, as if she were making quite sure that there could not be the slightest misunderstanding.

"Paul, I don't know what is worrying you. I don't know why you're lying. But you were at the Oval this afternoon and you caused that accident. I saw it with my own eyes. Jeremiah was killed, don't you understand? If the police find out it was you—"

"I tell you I wasn't there!"

There was another pause. Then: "I can't understand you," Bella Daventry said, wearily. "I just can't understand you. I *saw* you."

Silence came again, except for that strangely laboured, panicky breathing. Neither the man nor the girl spoke for a long time, which was measured not in seconds but in minutes. Rollison sidled closer to the door, intending to look into the room, hoping that he could see them both without being seen. He would probably recognise the back view of this Paul – the fair, curly head of the driver of the little car. He was as anxious to see his face.

He drew near the edge of the door.

Then the panting stopped, there was a gasp, a cry: *"Paul!"*

"I wasn't there, I tell you," the man cried. "You're lying, you want to get me hanged, you—"

"Let me go!"

"I wasn't there, the police can't find out unless you tell them. That's what you want to do, you want to get me hanged! Well—I won't let you. You'll never—"

"Paul!" she almost screamed. "Put that knife away. Put it—"

Rollison thrust the door back and rushed in, swift as a man could move. Suddenly, death was in the air, terror in the girl's voice. But it was a large room. The others were at the far end, a long way from Rollison; many tables and chairs were in the way.

The man named Paul, fair hair lit by the afternoon sun which poured through the window, was stabbing at Bella Daventry with a knife. The blade was not caught by the sun, but dull and deadly. And he held her fast with his left hand.

"Drop that!" roared Rollison, and leapt over a huge easy-chair.

But it was done before he could reach them, before they knew that he was in the room. It happened as swiftly as, on the green pleasaunce not far away, Trueman or Bedser hurtled the red ball down at the waiting batsman. The knife swept down towards the girl's breast. She screamed and struck out wildly, freeing herself, and turned the direction of the blow. Then, savage and powerful with desperation, she clutched at Paul's right wrist. He held the knife in his clenched fist like a dagger.

There was a moment of convulsive struggle while Rollison vaulted over a table, and drew within a foot of them. The girl's back was towards him, the man's face was twisted in frenzy. He tried to free himself, and the girl thrust desperately at his arm. The strength in her effort was so great that it turned the direction of the thrust.

For a second, the sun glinted on bright steel—

Then the point stabbed into Paul's throat. The blade slid in, and the glinting faded. There was just dull steel and a bone handle jutting out of the firm neck.

Bella Daventry said in a muffled voice: "No, oh, no." She hadn't turned to look at Rollison, who was holding her shoulders. She stared at Paul. The man, a young man with such golden hair, had fallen backwards, his legs crumpling, then his body folding. Now he lay with the knife sticking out of his neck, a knife with a fat, white slug of a bone handle. There was hardly any bleeding yet: the flesh was yielding where the blade had sunk in, and the blade was stemming the blood. Paul's eyes were half-closed and glazed, as a man's might be when death struck suddenly, giving him no chance. The nervous strength had left his body, he had become flaccid and powerless.

Dead?

"Oh, no, no, no," breathed Bella Daventry, "he can't be dead." She tried to move. Rollison's strong hands held her back, and for the first time she really began to look as if she knew that someone else was present. She stared at him. All the colour had left her cheeks, and that made the brilliance of her eyes greater and the scarlet of her painted lips like a daub of blood on vellum. Those lips were parted. Rollison could see her white teeth and the tip of her tongue. Recognition showed only vaguely in her eyes.

"He can't be dead!"

"Stand over there." Rollison pushed her towards a chair and the window. "Stay there, don't move." His voice was hard, emphatic. He let her go, turned towards Paul, and went down on one knee. As he did so, he pictured policemen in uniform doing this outside the Oval's iron gates, but that picture soon faded. He felt for Paul's pulse, in a limp, pale wrist.

He felt no beating.

Then blood welled up at the man's lips.

The girl uttered a sound, which was hardly intelligible, and moved forward. Rollison glanced round swiftly.

"Stay there."

She stopped, abruptly.

"Is he—is he dead?"

"I think so." Rollison was quite sure, but wanted to ease the shock a little. "There might be a chance—"

"He is dead," Bella Daventry said, and looked away from the man on the floor to Rollison. "Paul is dead, and I killed him."

"Keep your head." Rollison's voice was sharp; if he started to sympathise, she might break down completely. "He attacked you, didn't he? You were defending yourself. Just take it easy, and the police—"

Something in her expression told of the grip that horror had on her mind. He could imagine that she was staring into a strange, ugly future, a prospect which had not existed three minutes ago. She looked as she had when she had seen the accident and the other dead man; her stark and naked dread was an evil thing.

Rollison stood up, and took a brandy flask from his hip pocket. He filled the cap, and handed it to her. She stared at it, blankly. He put it to her lips, and she glanced at him; her beautiful blue eyes still held brilliance. Then slowly she put up a hand, cool in the thin cotton gloves, and held the cup and drank.

"Now sit down," Rollison said, "and I'll telephone for a doctor."

This wasn't so far from his own flat; he could rely on the discretion of his own doctor, if the man were in. Beyond that, he hadn't made up his mind what to do. He could understand the girl's horror, but he had seen what had happened, and could clear her from any serious charge. A scar would be left upon her mind, after the first effects had gone; but even the scar would fade.

How could he help her now?

The telephone lay on a small table near an armchair at the fireplace. He reached it, hesitated, then picked it up. Why not get the worst over quickly? He could dial Whitehall 1212, and bring the police here at once. A word with Superintendent Grice would make sure that the girl would have every consideration, and be quite free from all suspicion of murder. Grice would help to soothe her, a doctor would give her a sedative. When all that was over, the problem of Mr. McGinn and the two dead men could be tackled in earnest.

That was it; call Grice, at once.

Rollison actually started to dial.

Without giving him a moment of warning, Bella Daventry spun round from him and ran towards the door. She swerved past tables and chairs and a footstool with swift dexterity, and before Rollison had slammed the receiver back, she was at the door.

He was hemmed in by big chairs.

He pushed one out of his way and vaulted over another, clearing the still figure on the floor.

The door slammed.

He reached it, sliding to a stop, grabbed the handle and pulled – and jarred his arm badly. The door didn't open. He pulled again, tensing his muscles, but it stuck. It was locked. Even in that moment of crisis, part of the significance of that came home with a bump. Bella Daventry had been self-possessed enough to wait until he was at disadvantage, to run, and to close and lock the door.

He heard faint sounds, as of someone running.

He made himself back away from the door without haste, took out his knife and opened the pick-lock blade. But he needed seconds when he had none to spare, and hope of catching the girl was nearly gone.

As the door opened, another also opened on the landing below, and a deep voice came very loudly and very clearly:

"... not exactly fast scoring, but faster than England's average rate, so far, although it should be remembered that at Lord's and again at Leeds—"

The lower door closed.

Rollison reached the landing. A middle-aged woman was going down the bottom flight of stairs, grey-haired, spritely, carrying a shopping-basket. There was no sign of Bella Daventry. Rollison followed the woman swiftly, but made no sound that she could hear.

By the time she reached the front door, he was at the foot of the stairs. When she turned into the street, he was on the porch; but she did not know that he was present. She turned towards Brompton Road. Rollison forgot her, and looked about, but Bella Daventry wasn't in sight.

Not far along, parked in the middle of the street, was an olive-green Sunbeam Talbot.

Was it the car which had caused the Oval crash? He went along and peered inside, but the girl wasn't crouching down to hide from him. She had had time to reach the main street, and could have turned either way.

"Bella," Rollison said aloud, "I'd like a heart-to-heart chat with you, and then we'd see if you'd play angry."

No one heard him.

The deep, familiar voice came from an open window.

Rollison lit a cigarette, and went back to the house.

The girl had run away because of a fear which it might be easy to misunderstand. She had been as panic-stricken as Paul. It was easy to forget that Paul had drawn that knife, been prepared to kill her because she had seen him near the Oval; because he had believed that she wanted him to be hanged. Whatever the truth about Paul, he had been almost hysterical; a nervous wreck unable to control his thoughts, his fears, his movements.

Rollison could go off, saying nothing of what he had seen. Or he could telephone the police, and tell them everything. Or he could say that he had come into the flat to talk to Paul and found him dead; that way, he would not have to name the girl. It would not be according to the text-books. Jolly would most certainly disapprove, and the police – except, possibly, good friend Grice – would be likely to regard it as an indictable offence.

The girl would expect him to name her, and therefore would expect the police at her heels. If that didn't happen, she might talk much more freely to him, Rollison. Clearly she had some compelling reason to escape from the police; wasn't he more likely to find out what it was if he kept her secret? But if he did that, and told the police nothing about her, she would be in a bad spot if eventually they discovered that she had been here. A neighbour might have seen and recognised her.

If he told Grice now, he would be believed. If he waited, even Grice might think he was lying, so as to save the girl.

That didn't mean that his evidence was certain to be discredited. The police mattered less than the girl; it was important to win her confidence. He wanted to know more about the dead Jeremiah, dead Paul, Mr. McGinn, the girl's horror—

He had to tell the police something, for they would find his fingerprints.

There was no hurry.

Once back upstairs, he paused by Paul's dead body. The blood had flowed freely, the face was pallid.

Rollison dialled his flat.

It was some time before the call was answered, and when he heard the receiver come off, the next sound was not Jolly's voice but another, distant and yet clear; not deep and not English: Australian.

"... only another twenty minutes before tea, and as everyone knows, the tea break often unsettles a batsman. It's been an eventful afternoon, and let's face it, Australia have done very badly. Possibly the shower of rain at lunch-time—"

"This is the residence of the Honourable Richard Rollison," announced Jolly, with great precision; and the other voice became muted.

"Jolly—" began Rollison.

He could imagine that he startled Jolly. He was absently amused that Jolly, with his apparent disdain of such mundane things as Test Matches, should be listening in. But neither thing mattered so much as the sound he heard above Jolly's exclamation and above the muted Australian voice.

The front-door bell of this flat rang.

Chapter Five

Caller

"I am sorry if I seemed startled, sir," Jolly was saying, "I hardly expected—"

"Just a minute, Jolly." Rollison was sharp.

"Very good, sir."

Rollison raised his head, to listen. There was no other ringing sound. He put the receiver down carefully, stepped over Paul, and pushed past the chairs, to make quite sure that he had closed the front door. He had. He went back to the telephone, as the door bell rang again.

"Jolly," he said quickly.

"Sir?"

"I'm in a hurry. Do you know where to find Miss Daventry?"

"She gave an address, sir—she's secretary of a small firm of jewellers in Hatton Garden—Fingleton & Son. 217g Hatton Garden, if my memory serves me, and—"

"Lind out if she's often there. Find out her home address, if you can, and where she is now. Don't let anyone know who's inquiring. She's on the run from the police, and may have warned her friends not to talk. If you're quick you may get in first."

"I won't lose a moment!"

"And switch that radio off, hypocrite," breathed Rollison. Then hastily: "Hold on a minute!"

The front-door bell rang again.

He could see the door, and would be able to tell if anyone tried to force it, or used a key. And he would hear footsteps if the caller went away. He had time to give Jolly instructions.

"Jolly."

"I'm checking the name of the firm in the Directory, sir. It's here all right. And the number *is* 217g."

"Datas himself couldn't be better. Any news from Mr. McGinn?"

"None at all, sir. I went to the hotel, and the young woman was also waiting for Mr. McGinn. I—ah—got into conversation with her, and—"

"Gave her the card McGinn might have wanted," Rollison said dryly.

"Oh, no, sir." Jolly sounded scandalised, and then became bland. "I—ah—signed and wrote on another card, and kept the original."

Rollison said: "So you did," but did not refer to that again. "When you've done everything there is to do about her, check the Miramar and find out what else you can about McGinn. Hurry, Jolly."

"I will, sir!"

Rollison rang off, a smile checked because the front-door bell rang for a fourth time; the caller was persistent and patient. And presumably he wanted to see a dead man. Rollison moved towards the front door.

He heard footsteps.

A caller had given up, and was walking off. Rollison went closer to the door and opened it an inch or two, but when he peered out, the man had gone. Man? Or heavy woman? The footsteps were very heavy and deliberate. From the head of the stairs, Rollison looked down on a very big man descending the flight below.

In every way, the caller who had been disappointed was outsize. Even his hat was outsize – a ten-gallon hat of pale brown, with a curled brim on either side; a garish-looking hat. Anyone wearing it should also wear a gay satin shirt and a neckerchief, and be riding some spirited steed, miscalled a pony. But this man wore a suit of soft, smooth brown cloth. Rollison's view of him was foreshortened, but he could make out the large and quite remarkable stomach, covered by the flapping double-breasted coat; and the almost orange-coloured shoes, so highly polished that even in the shadowy light of the staircase and the hall, they gleamed brightly.

He reached the hall passage.

Had he looked up, he would have seen Rollison, but he did not look up.

He walked deliberately, heavily and yet not cumbersomely, out of the house.

Rollison went after him, slipped into the street, turned away from the big man who was so clearly an American, then turned after him. It was easy to pick out the massive man's car, a magnificent sky-blue Cadillac which looked as if a dozen chauffeurs had used a hundreds tins of Simoniz as well as much spit and polish to make a mirror-like surface.

A chauffeur dressed in green was getting out of the car. He was big and bulky, but not fat, like the other.

The fat man drew level, and the chauffeur touched his peaked cap.

"Where to now, Mr. McGinn?"

"I guess we'll go to the hotel," McGinn said, and the chauffeur opened the door for him to climb in.

Rollison walked on.

He had thought of using the Sunbeam Talbot to follow the Cadillac, but it wouldn't be necessary now. He had to telephone Grice, and see McGinn, but before that he had to search Paul's flat. There was a risk that McGinn would disappear again, but some risks had to be taken.

The Cadillac moved off.

Rollison hurried back to the flat. A middle-aged woman saw him going up the stairs. He smiled at her amiably, then rang Paul's bell, to make her think that the door was locked. She went into her own flat. Rollison slipped into Paul's, and set to work; and in moments like these Grice would have marvelled. There wasn't a corner that Rollison missed; the dead man's pockets, a desk, dressing-table drawers, likely places beneath the carpets, the wardrobe; everywhere. With expert eye and expert touch, he examined all likely hiding-places.

All he discovered was that Paul's surname was Wrightson, that he owed much money right and left, and that he worked for a firm of wholesale jewellers at 217g Hatton Garden. There were dunning letters, angry letters and threatening letters – and one note, piteous in its entreaty, from a girl whose child Paul Wrightson had fathered.

Here was all the evidence of a weak-willed man, desperately hard pressed; the kind who might, in desperation, do anything for money.

Well, Grice could find all this out for himself.

Rollison telephoned the Yard, and found Grice in and cheerful.

"If it's about McGinn, he's been back to his hotel," he said at once. "Sorry if I made you—"

"I don't know whether it's about McGinn or not," said Rollison, and the tone of his voice completely silenced Grice. "I've found a corpse, with a nasty hole in the throat. Much gone, too."

Grice almost bellowed: "Where are you? Come on, tell me, where—"

Rollison grinned.

"Easy, William, easy." He gave the address, and added almost cooingly: "I'd heard of this chap, and thought he might know something about McGinn. I found the flat door ajar, walked in and discovered the body. Quite a shock. Now I've an urgent job to do, so I'll be seeing you."

"You stay where you are!"

"But Bill," said Rollison chidingly, "I want to have a little chat with Millionaire McGinn."

He rang off, on Grice's almost angry order, looked round the room, stared thoughtfully at the dead Paul, who had been in so many difficulties which would worry him no longer, and then went out.

He hadn't seen a picture of Bella Daventry here, or seen the name Jeremiah.

He wanted to see Bella much more than he wanted to see McGinn; but McGinn would do for a start.

Outside, it was a different world again; of everyday people and bright eyes and men buying newspapers as swiftly as they came off the presses. At the corner with Brompton Road, a newspaper boy called: "More wickets tumble."

Rollison bought a paper, glanced at the score, and rejoiced. Eight wickets were down for two hundred and ten. He beckoned a taxi. Sitting back on his way to the Miramar Hotel and his flat, he felt an odd, unexpected and irrational moment of exasperation. He wanted to be at the Oval. A few hours ago he would have said emphatically that nothing would have kept him away on this day of all days. But it had; and he wouldn't go back.

There were two dead men …

Monday—

He lit a cigarette and closed his case with a snap, then turned firmly to the columns which did not report cricket. But he was soon lured back. For thirty thousand fans at Kennington and many millions on this isle, life was wonderful, only Lindwall was a danger now. The Aussies might be out for little more than two hundred, and the wicket wasn't bad; everyone agreed that the wicket wasn't bad.

He thrust the paper aside.

Why had Bella Daventry run away? She had seemed to be in a state of collapse, but had kept her wits about her, chosen the perfect moment to fly and to outwit him. No fool, that girl. She hadn't murdered Paul, although it could be said that she had killed him. But she knew there was a witness, so she should not have been afraid.

Her fear had really started when she had seen the man Jeremiah run down outside the Oval gates, and now it was easy to understand why she had been so horrified. For, like the van-driver and, with luck, like several other people, she had seen the little Sunbeam Talbot, driven by Paul. He had forced the van over, so making it run the unknown man down.

From then on, she had lived with fears. Pacing up and down the pavement. Stalking towards the flat. Facing Paul – and then realising that he was ready to kill her. She must have known that he wasn't really sane, that only a man living on his nerves would have made such an attack.

Why had she run?

And why had Mr. Millionaire McGinn come to see Paul Wrightson?

Mr. McGinn, said the porter at the Miramar, had just gone out, leaving word that he would not be back for several hours.

Rollison's flat was empty when he reached it.

He let himself in with a key, closed the door, and, almost by force of habit, had a look round in each room. It was nearly a quarter to six. The big-screen television set in a corner seemed as dead as a grey day. The small radio, on the desk, was silent now. Both radio and television would be transmitting the play at the Oval. He switched on the radio, almost absent-mindedly.

There was a message on the desk, in Jolly's copperplate handwriting:

Miss Daventry has a flat at 27 Rye Street, Chelsea – off the Embankment and not far from the Albert Bridge. She is secretary-director of Fingleton and Co., and the other directors are Jeremiah Fingleton, aged about 50, Paul Wrightson, aged about 30, and Arthur Rowe, whom no one seems to know. I am going to Rye Street and will report periodically by telephone.

P.S. Mr. McGinn has not telephoned again, sir.

Rollison smiled faintly. Bless Jolly. The radio came on, very softly; he didn't realise why it was subdued until he turned up the volume. Jolly had turned it down when the telephone call had come, and not used it again. Lindwall was batting with vigour, the score wasn't quite so good; two hundred-and-fifty-nine for nine. Bowler had turned batsman, these Aussies never knew when they were beaten. Bedser was bowling.

He switched off; an exercise in will-power.

So Jeremiah was a director of Bella Daventry's company, and she had seen him killed. That was explanation enough of horror. Paul Wrightson, a director of the same firm, had been responsible for Fingleton's death; his partner's death. He'd not actually killed

Jeremiah Fingleton, but his guilt had turned his mind. Bella had nearly died. Beautiful Bella. Where was she? Did she think she could stay free long? Was she – could she be – as desperate as Paul had been?

The telephone bell rang.

Rollison guessed right.

"Yes, Jolly?"

"I think you will agree that I made a satisfactory move, sir," Jolly said in a voice that was almost glib. "I came by taxi and retained it. Miss Daventry, carrying a large suitcase, is now walking from her flat towards the Embankment, obviously seeking another taxi. Shall I follow her?"

"Don't lose her, for ten fortunes!"

"I will do my best not to," Jolly promised gravely. "I really must go, sir, she is near the corner. Have you—?"

"Two-five-nine for nine."

"Oh, what a pity," said Jolly. "I'll report directly I have more news, sir."

Rollison put the receiver down, then went to the window and stood staring out. The trouble was simple; except for Bella Daventry and Mr. Millionaire McGinn, he didn't know where to start – unless it was on Fingleton & Company, of 217g Hatton Garden.

Well, why not?

The police would be there if Jeremiah had been identified; but if he hadn't, there might be no one at the office.

The radio and the television called and pleaded.

Rollison went out, heading for Hatton Garden, thinking of Bella and her wild rush away from him.

Chapter Six

Bella's Flight

Bella Daventry came out of the house where she lived, carrying a suitcase which was so heavy that even before she reached the road, it was weighing her down on one side. She looked up and down, quickly, almost fearfully. There was a street of terrace houses, not unlike those where Paul lived. *Had* lived. These were of reddish-brown brick, the windows were wider and they weren't so tall, but there was great similarity.

She turned towards the Embankment.

She saw a man turn into Rye Street, youthful, fair-haired, walking briskly and with long strides. She caught her breath. It wasn't Paul, it couldn't be Paul, but he had the same kind of hair, the same easy walk – he looked much as Paul had looked before disaster threatened them all.

The man turned into a house.

He stopped by the front door, making a pretence of searching for his key while he looked at Bella Daventry. She only noticed that he was staring at her. Everyone stared at her. From the moment she had fled from Paul's flat, every pair of eyes had been turned towards her, as if suspiciously or accusingly. She knew that it was nonsense, that these strangers did not even know that Paul was dead, but – they stared.

The young man actually took a step towards her. In any other mood she might have guessed the truth; that he was trying to pluck up courage to offer help with the case. In this mood, he made her heart beat faster and with suffocating thuds. Her head rose sharply, her pace quickened, she carried the case more easily for a few yards, passing the fair-haired young man. There were tears in her eyes – tears because she could see Paul's face, his glaring eyes when he had threatened her, the knife in his hand, and – the knife in his neck.

She felt as if his blood were flowing and choking her.

A car started up.

She glanced round, in sudden, unreasoning panic. It was a taxi, old-fashioned, looking like a shiny black box. She turned suddenly, swiftly, and raised her free left hand, but the driver took no notice, and she saw that his flag was down.

In the back of the taxi, out of sight, sat Jolly.

There were always taxis along the Embankment, but she didn't want to stop and wait, too many people would see her, and she was anxious not to be seen. She felt starkly conspicuous. She was tall and hated her height, beautiful and resentful of her beauty, because she knew that she would never be easily lost in a crowd.

Several men passed, most of them on the other side of the street, and stared at her.

A policeman came walking steadily, statelily. The suffocating beat at her heart was frightening. This pale-faced man, shorter than many, was on the Embankment side of the road, his helmet outlined against the silvered Thames. No craft of any kind rode on the calm water, which passed on gently, smoothly, inexorably – like this policeman.

He looked across at Bella.

In his uniform, it was easy to forget that he was just another man, and that few men could forbear to stare. She wanted to snatch up the case and run, but knew that it would be folly. Two people, man and woman, came out of a house just behind her, and one paused. Bella knew that they could hear her laboured breathing, and she tried to hold her breath.

They passed.

The policeman passed, too, but looked back at her.

A taxi came along, slowing down. She didn't realise what it was until it was almost on her.

"*Taxi!*" The word exploded, reaching the couple, the policeman and a dozen others, making Bella as noticeable as if she were in fancy dress. Cheeks almost scarlet, she lifted the case and pushed it into the cab, got in, said: "Waterloo, please," and almost fell back on to her seat. The taxi gathered speed smoothly. It passed an old-fashioned, square-topped cab, but she didn't notice that; she had eyes only for the policeman, who was still walking steadily, showing no interest in her now.

She leaned back and closed her eyes. That shut out the picture of the winding Thames, the bridges spanning it, the yellow-brown mass of the Battersea Power Station; but another picture came instead – of Paul, with the knife in his neck.

She shivered.

Then, slowly, deliberately, she made herself sit up and look about her. The brightness of the early evening reflected from the Thames and touched her eyes. From somewhere, she had found a needed strength. At traffic lights just ahead the taxi slowed down, and a newsboy called: "Test score, latest."

That sent her mind flashing back to the Oval, the courteous yet impatient young man who had shown her into the pavilion, the strikingly handsome Rollison who had been surprised and then, without any doubt at all, annoyed. Men and their games! At first she had been startled by his good looks and clean-cut features; he was an impossible Adonis of a man, yet for a moment his eyes had shown both admiration and understanding. Then, suddenly, they had frozen and she knew that he had wished her a thousand miles away from here.

Like pictures distorted by a kaleidoscope, the rest followed. Talking to him, leaving him, feeling rebuffed and angry, reaching the taxi, turning, seeing Paul, the little green car cutting across the van, forcing it on to the pavement and over – over Jeremiah.

Her nerves tightened again; were like wires, pulling through her flesh.

From that frightening scene her mind picture flashed to the flat, and Paul with the knife, hating her, accusing her – the desperate moments of fear. Then Rollison's hands firmly on her shoulders, Rollison giving her orders, holding the brandy in front of her lips, giving her a chance to steady herself, and to think – and then to act.

Well, she couldn't tell him; she couldn't tell anyone, yet.

He had a great reputation, though; she had often heard of him as a private detective, a fabulous person whom one heard and read about, but never met. Every now and again one of the newspapers would take up a case he was on, or there would be some *cause célèbre* involving him. He flashed across the headlines like a meteor.

Why had Connor McGinn gone to see him?

At least she was beginning to think more rationally.

That was an important question: why had McGinn gone to see a private detective?

She had been so busy with her thoughts that she did not realise that they had reached Parliament Square. The evening rush-hour traffic was thickening. The taxi was held up on the approaches to Westminster Bridge, and Big Ben boomed six deep, commanding notes, and fell silent, setting the cackling traffic free again. Newsboys were calling their one theme song. A car drew up alongside, and its radio was going.

"... just have to hand it to these Australians, they're not finished until the last man's out. There goes Lindwall, then, and the crowd's rising to him. What a fine knock it was! Well, that's given fresh heart to England. And in spite of a few fielding lapses, England has done a magnificent job. It's easy to forget that before play started, nearly every Englishman would have been satisfied to know that we'd have five wickets down for two hundred odd. Trueman's been magnificent, everything we hoped, of him. No words of praise are too great for Bedser. Bailey—"

The traffic moved off again, as a policeman's arm dropped. A taxi passed Bella Daventry's. She glanced at it, without thinking, and saw a small man with a bowler hat, his back towards her.

They crossed the bridge, his taxi just behind.

They swung left, leaving the squat solidity of London City Hall on one side, hiding the Thames and the pleasure boats and the distant silhouette of London's skyline.

They kept in the stream of one-way traffic, then turned off into Waterloo, and she could just see the bowler hat and a cheek of the little man; he had a wizened face. When the taxi stopped and she got out, the man was paying off his cab. She recognised him then – a man who had been at the Miramar; Rollison's servant.

She walked past him, behind a porter who made easy work of her suitcase. Three times she looked back, seeing Rollison's man once. He looked prim, neatly dressed in black coat and striped trousers, a little sad, almost lost in the mass of people thronging the platform. Nearly everyone seemed in a hurry.

The porter went to Platform 9.

Bella Daventry went to the suburban-line booking office, where there were long queues. Rollison's man was nowhere in sight.

She booked a return ticket to Heybridge.

Rollison sat back in his taxi as it passed 217g Hatton Garden. His hopes faded, for two uniformed policemen stood outside, and a Yard sergeant appeared in the side doorway. He was too late.

He did not even stop the cab, but frowned, feeling oddly frustrated; every move he made led to a dead-end.

At least Jolly was having better luck. And it was easy to forget how much he knew that he hadn't known a few hours ago.

It was ten past six when he reached his flat, and absently he switched on the television. He stood watching the screen. His heart gave a foolish leap when he saw Hutton and Edrich walking out to bat; so the Australians were all out.

The telephone bell rang. He moved towards his desk quickly, Jolly and the girl back in his mind again.

Paul had tried to kill the girl, remember.

He reached the desk and the telephone.

"Rollison speaking."

"This is Jolly, sir," Jolly said, quietly. "I am at Waterloo. Miss Daventry has booked a return ticket to Heybridge. She knew that I followed her to the station, but may think that I then lost interest. Shall I follow farther?"

"What's she look like?"

There was a brief pause; and it took a great deal for Jolly to pause in a search for words. Then he said very carefully and precisely: "Haunted, sir."

"Follow her," Rollison said abruptly. "Look after her, too. Let me know where she goes. Don't take any chances, if you think trouble's in the offing, call in the local coppers."

"Very good, sir. Have you any reason to believe that she is walking into trouble?"

"My enemies would call it a hunch," said Rollison, acidly.

"I will be very careful indeed," murmured Jolly. "Goodbye, sir."

Rollison heard him ring off, put the receiver down slowly, and didn't move. The commentator on the television was silent, the pictures flickered and reflected on a small glass case fastened to the wall behind the desk. Rollison stared at this, the trophy wall. The glass case contained five small, cylindrical phials of lethal poisons, once intended to kill a family of five. Rollison had followed a hunch, and saved all but one of the family. The whole wall was a story, in exhibits or trophies which some called souvenirs, of murder and attempted murder and narrow escapes; and not a few hunches were among them. But hunches could work two ways. There, at the top of the motley, was a top-hat with a bullet-hole through its sleek fur. He had worked on a hunch that there was no danger, on the night when a bullet had gone through that and shaved the top of his head.

He had no more liking for hunches than the next man, but he had them.

The television was behind him, and the trophies in front – knives, guns, knuckle-dusters, many kinds of lethal weapons, oddments which had no apparent connection with murder but had in fact the closest associations; and a hangman's rope, which many said had once hanged a man at Wandsworth Gaol. No one could explain how it had come into the possession of Rollison, and Rollison never attempted to enlighten anyone.

He was hardly aware of all these.

He was thinking of Jolly's long, deliberate pause; not only to search for the right word, but determined to impress.

"*Haunted*, sir."

That was exactly right; that was the word to explain the look in Bella's eyes when she had stared at the van and the crushed body of a man; that was the word to explain how she had looked when she had been standing and staring at dead Paul and the knife.

Jolly was good, but Jolly was old and much less limber than he had been. He, Rollison, ought to have gone himself; searching Paul Wrightson's flat hadn't paid dividends.

Hadn't it? He now knew that McGinn had called on Wrightson.

He moved from the telephone and looked at the television. Hutton played a backward defensive stroke. Then three things happened at the same time, jolting Rollison out of the mood of inexplicable apprehension.

The telephone bell rang.

The front-door bell rang.

Hutton, shown in close-up, shaped to the ball, which appeared like a dark dot, faltered, made a false stroke.

"Oh, that's a lucky one!" cried the commentator. "It isn't often that Hutton—"

The telephone bell kept ringing, and the front-door bell rang again. Those two things told Rollison how long he had stopped to watch the screen. He hurried to the front door, opened it without thinking, and stood squarely in front of a big man who had a green scarf drawn up over his face.

The apparition was utterly unexpected, as a thunderbolt, Rollison hadn't a split second of warning, hardly time for his mind to screech *danger.*

The man smashed a blow at his stomach, he hadn't a chance to avoid it. Pain went through him, growing into a swelling nausea. The big man pushed him back, closed the door, then hit him again, this time on the chin.

Rollison went down, sickeningly.

The telephone bell rang. *Brrr-brrr-brrr.*

The commentator on television was speaking steadily.

Chapter Seven

Big Fist

Rollison heard the sounds without understanding what they were. The nausea from the first blow was worsened by the pain from the second and by the blow on the back of his head as he fell. Then realisation came back, as he saw the masked face drawing nearer, saw a big fist, clenched and in front of his nose, and could do nothing to stop the blow.

The fist rapped him on the chin.

The man, on his haunches, drew his fist away and put his left hand into his pocket.

Rollison had a strange, distorted view of all this, and saw the scarf and the grey eyes of the stranger through a mist of pain and shock. His senses were still reeling, and he didn't try to move.

What was the man with the big fist doing?

Rollison tried to see. He was fiddling with both hands, now – as a man might who was pulling on a glove. Only this wasn't a glove. This was a knuckle-duster. It fitted snugly over the big fist, a brassy, dirty-yellow thing, which looked murderous. It had blunted spikes all over it. Two or three blows in the face from that, and his cheeks would be lacerated, the bone laid bare.

The man worked his fingers about when the thing was on, then moved with a stabbing jab at Rollison's cheek. Rollison jolted his head back, and cracked it on the floor again. The fist missed by inches. He knew that the man had intended to miss; had meant only to frighten.

He hadn't yet spoken.

He moved his left hand, grabbed Rollison's coat lapels, and hauled him to his feet. Only a man with very powerful arms could have done that. He held Rollison upright, and sneered. It was hellish to feel so helpless; but at least there was some breathing space, and the nausea wasn't so bad.

Suddenly the man pushed Rollison powerfully, the flat of a massive hand hard against his chest. Rollison steadied; the palm thwacked him again; he had to keep going back. The powerful pushes with the flat of the big man's hand were painful, but that wasn't the kind of pain that mattered.

At last Rollison stood with his back to the inside wall of his own hall. His assailant was two inches taller than he, which made the man six feet three; he was enormous across the shoulders, too. He wore an old raincoat, which was unnecessary today, and his eyebrows were very black, thick and false. The only part of the face which Rollison could see was the eyes.

The man hadn't yet spoken.

He backed a pace, so that he stood four feet from Rollison, looking him up and down.

The telephone bell had stopped ringing, but now and again the voice came from the television. A clock struck the quarter, and the clear, tinkling clock-bell echoed for a long time.

"What did you take from Wrightson's place?" the man demanded, and his hard, metallic voice gave him away.

He was McGinn's chauffeur. Sitting in the Cadillac, this man could easily have seen him come out of Wrightson's street door, in McGinn's wake.

Who else knew he had been to Wrightson's flat?

"Come on—talk." That hard voice was menacing; so was the raised fist with the spiked knuckle-duster. The man had only to lunge forward, in order to lacerate Rollison's cheek and scar him for life. He was standing with his feet apart, ready to lunge, but obviously sure that Rollison wouldn't put up a fight.

Rollison moistened his lips. "I've never—"

"I saw you, don't lie to me." The man moved, swift as a striking snake. Rollison's breath almost screamed inwards. The knuckle-duster fist came straight and savage, not to the face but to the chest, and the pain was like the savage bite of a flame-thrower.

"You heard me. What did you take?"

"Nothing!" It wasn't difficult to sound terrified. "Nothing at all!" The difficulty was to *think,* to find a way of fighting back.

"What were you doing there?"

"I—I'd been following—" began Rollison, and caught his breath. He must not name Bella Daventry. Jolly was looking after her, but what hope would Jolly have against ruthlessness like this?

"Listen, Rollison," the big man growled, "talk fast—if you ever want to see McGinn alive."

Sweat stood out on Rollison's forehead, on his neck and lips; and veins in his throat and forehead were like cords, too, and one was pulsing away as if sharing his desperation. *Think, think, think!* Fool the brute.

"Forget McGinn, and remember your friends won't recognise you again if you don't talk," the big man demanded. "Why go to see Wrightson?"

"I'd talked—to McGinn!" Rollison's words came out like scalding steam. He mustn't name the girl, that was all- important; keep this menace from her. "McGinn—McGinn had mentioned Paul Wrightson, said he'd want me to go and see him."

"For why?"

"I don't know." The man glared. "*I don't know!*" breathed Rollison.

"So you don't know," sneered the big man. "Poor Torf—you don't know. Lemme see if I can help you. When did you hear from McGinn?" He smoothed the knuckleduster with a horny palm.

That was easy.

"He rang up this morning. I said I'd see him here. He was coming at half-past ten. He didn't turn up." Rollison uttered each sentence very carefully and roundly, as if his life depended on being believed; quite possibly it did, he knew. But he was feeling easier, and thinking was possible again. Had the brute come with intent to kill? Forget it.

He hadn't named the girl, that was a trick to him. And—

"Seen Bella Daventry, since she went to the Oval?" That sounded almost as if the man could read his thoughts. The worst thing about him was his complete assurance; he not only knew what he was doing, but also seemed capable of carrying out everything he planned.

"No!" Rollison said; too abruptly?

"She come here?"

"No." That was better; less vehement.

"What did she want?"

"She wanted to know if I'd seen McGinn." Rollison looked squarely into the big man's eyes. He didn't move his arms or shoulders, but was relaxed; he was measuring the distance between them, reckoning the chances of landing a blow hard enough to hurt. If he tried and failed, that knuckle-duster—

His chest still burned.

"What else did she want?"

"That was all."

"You see her since?"

Here was the dangerous, perhaps fateful moment; his questioner might know he had seen her again.

"No." He was proud of his composure.

There was no change in the expression of the cold grey eyes.

"That had better be true," the man said. "Now listen, Torf. You've had plenty of breaks. You've stuck your nose in where it wasn't wanted too often. Don't do it again. Keep out of this job. It's between some friends of mine and the Yank McGinn, and it stays that way. If we run into the cops, okay, that's an occupational risk, but we aren't taking any chance with you. Understand?"

"I told McGinn I couldn't take on anything," Rollison said, with a kind of false calm, "I refused to do anything next week. I've every intention of being at the Oval—"

"You won't be at the Oval," the big man said. "You won't be anywhere but here, unless it's in a nursing home. Or a morgue. Because I'm going to beat you up, see. I'm going to pay you back for all the times you've stuck your nose in where it wasn't wanted, and when I've done your nose won't be so flicking straight and aristocratic." He was poised, the knuckle-duster only a foot away from Rollison's face, fist held as if he were at the start of a round in the square ring. "You're going to know what it feels like to be cut to ribbons, see? You're going——"

Rollison said: "Why don't you cut the cackle and get going?"

The grey eyes narrowed, as anger touched them.

"You're good at talking," the man sneered. "You want to see what——"

He slashed a blow at Rollison's chin. Rollison swayed. The blow missed by a hair's breadth. Rollison could have hit back, or kicked, but he was off his balance, and the big man recovered, swift as a practised fighter.

The telephone bell rang, sudden, sharp, clear.

It made the big man relax for a split second, his eyes shifted towards the instrument on a table, his raised fists drooped. This was the moment of hope. Rollison kicked out, putting all his sinewy strength into driving his foot at the pit of the man's stomach. It went home, savagely. The man reeled back, turning colour. Rollison leapt, grabbed his right arm as he fell, actually heard a muted scream from the taut lips. Rollison twisted again. The big body was heaved over, the man thudded down on his face, one arm held behind him. Rollison forced the arm up towards his neck, then knelt on the small of the man's back. With that hold on him, even a gorilla would have had little chance.

Sweat dropped off Rollison's forehead; made his shirt damp at his back and neck. His collar was wet, and sweat ran into his eyes and trickled between his parted lips. He was breathing hard; hurtfully. He knew that he could not maintain the grip for long, that he was almost out on his feet. But he had to win now or go right under.

The telephone kept ringing.

He heard a voice, and it startled him; then he realised that it came from the television.

He struck a savage blow, the edge of his hand chopping on the thick neck. The big man grunted and sagged, his nose banged on the floor; he went out as clean as a whistle.

The telephone bell wouldn't stop ringing, but the commentator had stopped talking.

Rollison rested for a moment, kneeling on the big man's back, and then stood up slowly. He was trembling slightly. He drew his sleeve across his wet forehead, then pulled his handkerchief out of his pocket, dabbed his eyes and lips, and moved unsteadily towards the telephone. Damn the thing, why wouldn't it stop?

He hadn't long to work in; the man wouldn't be unconscious for more than a few minutes.

Damn the telephone!

He went unsteadily into the big room where the trophy wall seemed to sway up and down and the top-hat with the bullet-hole in it swayed to and fro, as if its invisible wearer was tipsy. *Damn* the telephone. The picture on the television screen was blurred; that was because of the sweat filming his eyelashes. He wiped them clean. By then he was at his desk, and groping for a bottle in one cupboard; brandy. There was a small glass. He took bottle and glass out.

The telephone bell wouldn't stop, and there was an extension in here. He glared at it, and tossed down brandy.

"Why the hell don't you stop ringing?" *he screeched.*

It didn't.

He gave a little sniggering laugh, and said with almost drunken solemnity: "Richard, you are slipping." Then, with the exaggerated care of a drunken man, he went into the small kitchen, which Jolly kept not only in meticulous order but also as spick and span as any ship's galley, took out a roll of cord, and went with this to the hall.

The bell was louder in here.

"Why the hell—"

The man lay limp, with one arm under him and the other lying loosely by his side. He would know all about that hold, next day; it would be days before his arm was free from pain, weeks before the bruises had gone.

"Wrists first," Rollison said to himself, as if he were reciting some lesson well learned. "Then his ankles, and if that ruddy telephone doesn't stop soon—"

He finished tying the man up; the telephone bell was still ringing. He went across the room, unsteadily. At the desk he nearly fell. The telephone stopped, a blessed relief; but in a few seconds it started again. He lifted the receiver slowly, effortfully, formed his words and spoke very slowly.

"This is Richard Rollison."

"Is that Mr. Rollison speaking?" a man asked.

He had an American voice.

Chapter Eight

Young Mr. McGinn

The voice wasn't Connor McGinn's, wasn't even like it. But unmistakably it was American.

Rollison didn't respond at once; the sense of shock over this trivial thing told him how badly his nerves had been shaken up.

"Are you on the line?" the man asked.

"Yes. Yes—this is Richard Rollison speaking." He hoped he sounded natural.

"Oh, that's fine! Mr. Rollison, I don't like to worry you, but I'm a little anxious about my uncle, and I thought maybe you could help me to find him. I'm speaking of Mr. Connor McGinn. My name is Rory McGinn. Do you happen to know where I can find my uncle?"

With an effort, Rollison said: "No, I'm afraid not."

"Have you seen him today?"

"No," said Rollison, and thought fleetingly of McGinn's visit to Paul's flat. Forget it. He didn't want to talk about McGinn. He watched his victim, thinking that when the huge shoulders began to move, it wouldn't be long before the hulk became a major threat again. "I'm sorry, I can't help you." The man on the floor had talked about McGinn, remember. "I—"

"Mr. Rollison," said young Mr. McGinn earnestly, "will you do me a very great favour, and allow me to call on you? I'd very much like—"

"Mr. McGinn, I'm sorry," Rollison said quickly, for the big man. was stirring. "I've an urgent call to make. I may be here at my flat at half-past eight. Call again, or come in person. Sorry I can't wait now."

"You're very good, Mr. Rollison. Thank you. I'll be there."

"Very well. Goodbye." Rollison put the receiver down sharply.

The big assailant was moving, and might soon try to get up. Rollison went to him, checked the cords, and at last began to feel that he could take things easily.

The man now lay on his side.

A voice said:

"... and then had light stopped play. No one was surprised, for the light had been getting gradually worse. England one run for no wicket, then, in reply to Australia's two hundred and seventy-five—"

Rollison moved forward, bent down, and studied his captive's face.

It was big, square and florid; one glance was enough to tell that the man had brute strength and brutish ways. He had a big, square jaw, a short upper lip carrying a slight scar, the shape of a half-moon, just beneath a broad nose with big, swelling nostrils. His hair was greying, and grew well back on his forehead; there was a sharp line of demarcation between the tanned and the white skin of his forehead, showing that he usually wore a hat. His left ear was almost a cauliflower; there wasn't much doubt that he'd been a bruiser. And he could still leave his mark on most men.

Undoubtedly, it was McGinn's chauffeur.

He hadn't come round yet, but was breathing gustily. The eyelids flickered, drawing attention to the short eyelashes. Only the eyebrows were false, obviously stuck on simply to hide the shape of his real ones. Rollison pulled them off, and found another scar beneath one of the false brows.

He went into a small boxroom, a kind of laboratory-cum-dark-room and Jolly's joy. He took a camera and fitted a flashlight, then returned and took two photographs of his victim. Next, he took out his gold cigarette-case, rubbed it clean of his own prints with a handkerchief, and placed it in the prisoner's hand. That made clear prints.

Moving very deliberately, he took the case into the study and put it on the desk, returned to the hall and went through the man's pockets.

One of the first things he found was a folded card, about eight inches by five. That brought a rueful frown to Rollison's forehead, for it was an Oval score-card for this day's match. There were the lists of the two teams of cricketing giants, the details of the play before lunch had been filled in, in large but neat writing. So had the first wicket after lunch – *Hassell c. Evans, b. Bedser.*

In a foolish way, Rollison half wished that he hadn't found this. It smeared a game which—

Idiot!

He found nothing that helped with identification. The wallet was empty except for a few pound notes, obviously the man had meant to make sure that he couldn't easily be identified.

Rollison stood up.

"It won't be easy to make him talk, either," he said *sotto voce.* "I wonder if Grice—"

That was the moment when he was back to the swift and calculating tempo that friends expected and enemies feared. Grice ought to have been here by now; or at least sent a man to question him. Grice wouldn't stay away much longer. There might be other callers. Rory McGinn might not observe the time stipulation; if he were anything like his uncle, he would expect the rules to stretch for him.

"Now we'll really get a move on," Rollison exhorted himself.

He could grin.

He felt better physically, too; the brandy had worked wonders.

He dragged the big man by the shoulders into Jolly's small bedroom, approached along a narrow passage and on the other side of the kitchen. He checked the cords again and, to make sure of the man, used his own scarf to gag him. Then he went through his pockets, to check that he had looked at everything.

He had; nothing told him this man's name.

He left him on Jolly's celibate bed, and closed the door without locking it. Then he went into the bathroom. He was sticky with sweat. He stripped and stepped under the shower, taking it cold. It stung and invigorated. He grabbed a towel, and was agreeably surprised at his own liveliness – until he rubbed his chest, without looking at what he was doing; it felt as if he had drawn a file across his bare skin.

He leaned forward, to look into the mirror.

There was the mark of the knuckle-duster, red where the skin had been punctured, pinky blue round the edges – rather like the spore of some great animal whose claws had gone in like spikes. That sobered him. He finished towelling and, with Jolly's voice sounding as if it were in his ear, rubbed in a salve; it stung for a bit. He changed vest, trunks and trousers, and slipped into a short-sleeved dark- blue shirt.

He was ready; and much, much better. Almost human.

He didn't waste time going to see the big man again. If the brute could be made to talk, it wouldn't be just yet. Rollison went into the living-room-cum-study, and saw a blank screen. He switched off, giving cricket hardly a thought.

What had the brute come for? To find out what he knew – or whether he had taken anything from Paul Wrightson's flat? Or to utter that warning about McGinn?

McGinn had told his chauffeur to go to the Miramar; and he'd never turned up. Why? Where had he been all day? Why had he gone to Wrightson's flat?

Sitting at his desk, smoking, a whisky-and-soda for strength and company, Rollison found himself going over all that had happened. He kept coming back to Bella Daventry; wishing that Jolly would call. So much time had been lost.

For the first time, he found himself wishing that he had gone to the Miramar instead of to the Oval. That was almost treasonable.

He finished his cigarette and lit another, took a drink, and stared at the blank television set. He wanted to bellow at the telephone, to will Jolly to call.

The bell rang.

He grabbed and answered—

"Stay there, Roily," Grice said brusquely. "I want to talk to you."

Rollison heard footsteps without being positive that they belonged to the Yard man. He went to the front door, holding a gun in his left pocket. He opened the door from one side, and glanced swiftly out, recognised Grice, then opened the door wide.

"Expecting trouble?" Grice asked, sardonically.

"Hasn't it come?" murmured Rollison, and was bland. He enjoyed being able to be bland. He kept remembering that about an hour ago he had felt as if his last moment had come.

Grice said: "So you're feeling smart, I wonder how long that will last," and sniffed as he went into the big room.

Rollison followed, closing the door firmly. Beyond two walls and a few cubic feet of space was the prisoner; and Grice need be told nothing about him. Grice was tall, a broad yet a spare-looking man, with big bones and little flesh. His cheeks were inclined to be hollow. His skin was sallow, as if he had come fresh from the mountains of Switzerland and their hot sun; the skin stretched so tautly across his nose that at the bridge it was almost white. He had fine brown eyes, an easy manner, easy, confident movements. One side of his face had a big burn scar; he and the Toff had been together when that had been caused, and Grice had been nearly blinded.

"Take a chair," Rollison offered, and hospitably: "What will you have? Anything from—"

"Lime juice, thanks."

"Listen, Bill, it won't do. Scotland Yard men were never intended to be teetotallers, and—"

"It might do you good if you were to drink less," growled Grice, who could be almost narrow-minded on the subject of hard liquor.

Rollison handed cigarettes, a book of matches and lime-juice-and-soda, then mixed himself a stiff whisky. So they eyed each other, smoked, and sipped until at last Rollison beamed.

"What was close of play?" he inquired.

"Two-seventy-five all out, and we—" began Grice, and then clamped on his words. "You know, you devil. And I'm not here to talk about cricket. Who killed Paul Wrightson?"

"Not I," said Rollison. "Not even with my bow and—"

"What were you doing at his flat?"

"Investigating."

"Don't play this funny."

"All right, Bill," Rollison said, changing his tone. "McGinn telephoned me this morning. He wanted to see me, I played hard to get, and he asked if I knew Wrightson. He said that he wasn't sure if Wrightson could be trusted." Rollison paused, to draw at his cigarette; and felt satisfied that Grice had swallowed this most plausible story. So far, so good. "McGinn was coming to see me, and didn't turn up. I checked the hotel, then thought that it might be worth seeing Wrightson. I've told you what happened then."

"Why didn't you stay at the flat?"

"Someone came to the door, and I wanted to follow him."

"Who was he?"

"I don't know—he got away before I saw him."

"Just like any figment of your vivid imagination," growled Grice. "Listen to me. McGinn's an American citizen. That lifts this job out of the ordinary. Don't make any mistake—"

Rollison let smoke trickle out of his nostrils.

"Scotland Yard all anxious to make sure we don't have any international incidents, eh? I'm with you all the way. But I haven't seen him. He didn't turn up here, and he didn't turn up at the Oval."

Grice said: "You almost convince me."

"It's gospel."

"I don't know whether to be pleased or sorry. You know he's disappeared, of course."

"Oh, I don't know. He went off once, but he came back, and—"

"The second time he was shanghaied," Grice said, and added bitterly: "Under the nose of one of my men. He was hit over the head and driven off in his own car—a Cadillac. We've a call out, of course."

"Well, well," breathed Rollison. "How's your man, Bill?" he added sweetly.

"He got a crack over the head, too."

"Can he identify the slugger?"

"Big, bearded man," said Grice, disconsolately. "And as powerful as a bruiser." He eyed Rollison thoughtfully, then went on: "Seen anyone else on this business?"

"I've heard a young man with a Harvard voice, who rang up to ask if I would see him, and made the same kind of suggestion as you—that McGinn had vanished. Any idea why?"

Grice leaned forward, stubbing out his cigarette. Rollison, who knew him well, believed that Grice was satisfied with his story. He was committed to it, now; if the police discovered that Bella Daventry had been to Wrightson's flat, it wouldn't be so good; but why cross bridges that might never be built?

"Did you know that McGinn is a collector of precious stones?" Grice demanded.

"Jolly said something about it. You said he was here with a fortune in jewels. Big or little fortune?"

"About one hundred and twenty-five thousand pounds worth," Grice said, with great deliberation.

"Really?" Even Rollison's voice squeaked.

"No doubt at all. He bought them in Spain, Italy and France, declared them to Customs when he came into the country, everything was square and above-board. His nephew's worried, in case he's been shanghaied for them. Was it the nephew, Rory McGinn, who telephoned you?"

"Yes. Don't tell me that McGinn carries a fortune like that about with him."

"He has been known to," Grice said, "but his nephew isn't sure about whether he's doing it this time. McGinn told no one where he put the jewels, and there was some sense in that. But there's no way of telling whether he had a fortune on him when he was kidnapped. Interesting, isn't it?"

"Very," Rollison said, and positively meant it. "I suppose you know that Wrightson worked for a small firm of jewel—"

"—merchants," Grice completed for him, and his voice changed slightly; it became harder. "Yes, I know. Paul Wrightson was a director of the firm. So was a man named Jeremiah Fingleton. Fingleton is also dead."

"What?"

"Now you're playing innocent," Grice said, and his voice hardened. "Listen to me. Not all policemen are fools, and one of these days you'll get a shock through refusing to admit that. The sergeant on duty outside the main gates at the Oval this afternoon recognised you, knows you ducked back and then came out again, pretending not to have seen the accident. But you saw it. He told me he thought it would be a waste of time questioning you himself, so he reported to his Divisional chief."

Straight-faced, Rollison said: "The only coppers I ever laugh at are C.I.D. chaps of high rank. What's all this adding up to, Bill?"

"You saw Jeremiah Fingleton run down and killed. You were at Wrightson's flat about the time he was killed, too. You saw Wrightson cause that crash, recognised his car, and went hell-for-leather after him. Was he alive or dead when you reached his flat?"

Rollison said very softly: "Dead, Bill."

"Did you see the woman there?" barked Grice.

Chapter Nine

Police Activity

Rollison, half-prepared for the question, resisted it, fought back the impulse to tell the truth, and wondered if he were being crazy. But he'd lied already, and before he told the whole truth, he wanted to see Bella.

He was worried about Bella; and Jolly. The telephone had been silent for a long time.

"What woman?" he demanded.

"Did you see one there?"

"An old soul—"

"This one wasn't old. You saw her at the Oval."

Yes, Grice was good, and he'd been playing a cunning hand. The ordeal of the struggle with the big man had taken a lot out of Rollison – and it was never easy to fool Grice. But he'd try, because he wanted to talk to Bella.

He wanted to hear that telephone, too.

"What's the matter with you?" demanded Grice. "Going deaf? I checked on you at the Oval. A woman answering the description of Bella Daventry went to see you and left just as Fingleton was killed. She was secretary-director of Fingleton's. Two of her co-directors have died of violence this afternoon. Was she at Paul Wrightson's flat when you got there? Come on, Sir Galahad, let's have the truth. She's *been* there. She was seen leaving in a hell of a hurry. Did you tell her to beat it, and promise to save her pretty neck?"

The telephone kept silent.

Rollison's lips curved faintly. He moved to pour himself out a drink, very conscious of Grice's commanding gaze. Grice was on top, and knew it. Two of Bella Daventry's co-directors were dead. There was a killer-type unconscious in the next room.

"She was there," Rollison said, and saw Grice relax, felt a little easier himself. There were limits to what he could do. "She didn't kill him, Bill. He tried to kill her. She'd seen what happened at the Oval, and he was almost demented. She accused him of killing this Jeremiah, and he pulled a knife. She struggled, and he stuck it into his own neck. I saw it all, but couldn't stop it."

He finished his drink.

The telephone was a black, silent Buddha.

Grice said: "I'm glad you've some sense. Where did she go?"

"She ran out on me."

"Not at your best, were you?"

"I can improve."

"Who called at the flat—or was that a decorative lie?" There was nothing he could do to save Bella Daventry from police interrogation, now, but he didn't have to name McGinn. The American might turn up again soon, preferring not to tell the police he had visited Wrightson's flat. Rollison needed some shots in his locker, too; so far, they were precious few.

"I didn't see who it was, Bill."

"Do you know where Bella Daventry is?"

"No," said Rollison, and had no difficulty in making himself sound convincing. "I wish to hell I did."

"Why?"

"She's terrified."

"Sure?"

"Quite sure."

"Listen," Grice said, "you might be telling the truth about Wrightson's death. I don't know. But don't waste any sympathy on Bella Daventry. Don't let a face and figure fool you. She needs money—the whole firm of Fingleton's does. The firm has been buying and selling stolen jewels. Yes—that's a fact. McGinn's a big collector. His nephew isn't—but recently his nephew's been very friendly with a certain Bella Daventry. If ever there's been a conspiracy to defraud, this is it."

Rollison didn't speak.

"Know Arthur Rowe?" Grice flung out.

"~~Who?~~"

"Arthur Rowe."

"Never heard of him."

"Sure?"

"Bill, I've been an improvement on George Washington." Grice relaxed with a grin.

"Possibly," he conceded, "but I'd need a lot more proof. A certain Arthur Rowe is the fourth and only remaining director of Fingleton's. I can't find anyone who's set eyes on him, but there hasn't been much time to look. There will be. He has an accommodation address in London, and we're after his real address. Bella Daventry may have gone to him."

"Isn't she at *her* house?"

Grice didn't give any sign at all that he suspected the integrity of that question.

"No. I've been there. She'd looked in, grabbed a few clothes, and ran off. Know where she is?"

"No," said Rollison.

They both grinned.

"Where's Jolly?"

Rollison burst into a laugh.

"Bill, you're on form tonight! He's out looking for Bella. If he finds her, I'll let you know."

There was a long pause. Then: "Mind you do," Grice said. "But we're better at finding things. We found McGinn's Cadillac undamaged, in a side street. No prints, they'd been wiped off."

So there was peace between them.

Grice left soon afterwards.

The black Buddha of a telephone kept silent.

Rollison couldn't keep still. He walked the flat, contemplated the prisoner, who was conscious and looked murderous, studied the trophy wall, kept glancing at the telephone.

He could have turned his prisoner over to Grice. Could have – or should have? He wasn't working for McGinn, he'd no client to serve, there might be nothing in this for him. Why hold out on Grice over anything?

It was partly the fear in Bella Daventry's eyes.

It was partly McGinn's booming request for help.

It was chiefly the snapping of his own conscience. They'd asked for help, he had rebuffed them. If he'd seen McGinn instead of going to the Oval, a lot of this might not have happened. He didn't make the mistake of blaming himself; but he wanted to hit back, to make amends.

And if Bella would talk, the rest might fall into place.

If it didn't, he could work on the prisoner.

Suddenly, he swung round, went into the dark room, dusted and photographed the prints on his cigarette-case, and then developed the negatives. It gave him something to do.

He had finished, and had two prints of the big man's face and fingerprints drying, when the black Buddha spoke from the other room.

"I'm speaking from a call-box at the corner of River Walk and The Green, Heybridge," Jolly said, with a calmness which drove urgent fears away. "She has gone to a bungalow fronting the river, one called Fingleton. The house appeared to be empty when she arrived, I can see no evidence that anyone else is there. Shall I make inquiries about the tenants or occupiers, sir, or shall I keep the bungalow under surveillance?"

"Watch the place," Rollison said swiftly. "I'll come at the double."

"Very good, sir."

"I'll try to bring some help," Rollison added. "Look out for Bill Ebbutt's men."

"I will sir," Jolly said, and sounded relieved.

Rollison rang off, lit a cigarette, and lifted the telephone again, all without a pause. He was feeling much, much easier in his mind, but the girl's horror had not been imagined, McGinn had been kidnapped, if there was one killer-type like his prisoner, there might be others.

He dialled a Whitechapel number, which rang for long seconds before the ringing sound stopped.

"'Oo is it?" asked a man in a Cockney voice.

"Didn't see you at the Oval today, Bill," said Rollison, in his mildest manner.

There was a pause; then an eruption.

"Caw strike a light, it's Mr. Ar. 'Ere, Mr. Ar, wot a day! Bury me quick if I didn't think we was going to get 'em aht for under two 'undred. I don't mind telling yer, there's bin plenty on the 'ouse tonight, and if we lick the Aussies it's free drinks all round while I got a drop o' beer left in any barrel. 'Appy as a sandboy, our boys—but Mr. *Ar?*"

"Yes, Bill."

"You wasn't there, was you?"

"I had a case, Bill."

"You 'ad—" began Bill Ebbntt, who was speaking from a small cubby hole – called by courtesy and the proprietor an office – in his gymnasium near the Mile End Road. Close by was the Blue Dog, a public-house managed with remarkable efficiency by the same Bill Ebbutt; and Rollison knew that in the gymnasium, now, young hopes were slapping each other with leather gloves, or punching balls, or vaulting horses or doing a hundred and one other things to keep themselves fit and to justify the faith and confidence that Big Bill Ebbutt placed in them.

Ebbutt and Rollison shared a love of boxing and a love of cricket among many other things. Few men were better known in the East End of London than the Toff, none was more welcome in Ebbutt's pub or Ebbutt's gymnasium. They had a singular identity of outlook, in that they usually understood exactly what inspired the other to do this thing or the next. But some things were incomprehensible.

"You 'ad a case wot kept you from the Oval ter*day,*" breathed Ebbutt, in a strained voice; then it grew loud and shook with laughter. "You're kidding, strike a perishing light'n I fell for it! Nar be serious, Mr. Ar. Wotja fink of Trueman? Mind you, that Lock's the lad for my money, 'im and Laker—"

"Two murders, Bill."

There was a pause; somewhere in the background were slapping sounds, telling of the hopefuls who were still in the ring. Then came Ebbutt's voice, which had suddenly become creaky.

"So you want some 'elp, do you?"

"A lot, I think."

"Well, I'm always willin'," Ebbutt said, still creakily, "but I'm not so sure abaht the ovver boys if it lasts over till Monday. Tomorrow's all right, except that my Liz and Charlie's old china don't like us 'itting the beef on Sundays, but Monday—I dunno. They gotta queue up, yer know. Ten of them was in their places at four o'clock s'morning to make sure of a decent seat. Still, I needn't talk to you, Mr. Ar. Wot's cookin'?"

"Two good men and true tonight, Bill, at the flat. I'm going to try an old trick. And three or four at a place on the Thames, Heybridge. Do you think you can round them up right away and get them moving?"

"Matter o' raisin' me voice," Bill Ebbutt said simply, "that's all. I got me pencil, wot's this address at Heybridge?"

Rollison told him; and could imagine the slow-moving pencil gripped tightly in fat fingers, the tongue poking out at one corner of the full, generous lips of the ex-bruiser. He gave Bill Ebbutt plenty of time to finish.

"Expectin' trouble tonight?" asked Ebbutt, at last.

"Could be. Jolly's about at Heybridge, he'll brief you. I hope to be there later."

"Look, Mr. Ar," urged Bill Ebbutt, loudly and gustily, "let's hit 'em for six ternight. Get it all over an' done wiv, then we can all go along to the Oval on Monday light-'earted. Can't we?"

Rollison chuckled. "I'll try and hit that six," he promised. "Thanks, Bill. I'll be seeing you."

When he rang off, it was a quarter to eight. He was happier but hungry. Rory McGinn might come soon. There was a possibility of getting urgent news from Jolly before Ebbutt's men reached here or reached Heybridge, but he had to wait for Ebbutt's men. He was fidgety, edgy and conscious of the fact that he hadn't fully recovered from the big man's vicious attack.

It would be a long time before he forgot opening the door to the man. He didn't want to question him yet, there wasn't time to make a job of it.

He found some ham in the larder, and prepared a snack. It was twenty minutes past eight when he had finished. No one had arrived. Who'd get here first – McGinn's nephew or Ebbutt's men?

Suddenly, footsteps sounded on the stairs, running footsteps. Rollison moved swiftly into the hall, worked almost by his own reflexes. The footsteps drew nearer, carrying some urgent message. And carrying fear? Everything but this was forgotten, now – the prisoner, Bella, missing McGinn, Ebbutt—

The door bell rang. A fist thumped on the door. A man cried: "Let me in, let me in!"

Chapter Ten

Rory McGinn

Rollison reached the door as the man called out again. The voice was American, and seemed to carry desperate fear. "Let me in, let me in!" But there was no other sound, no suggestion of pursuit, and Rollison had been caught once tonight.

He kept his left hand round the automatic in his pocket, and opened the door from one side, more slowly than for Grice. The bell rang sharply again.

"Let—me—in!"

There was light in the landing, showing the figure of a man close to the door, head turned towards the stairs as if he were staring into horror. Rollison opened the door a fraction wider; and there was a second man, on the stairs, coming up slowly, with a knife in his hand. It was like a still from a suspense film. The man coming up the stairs was small, crouching, masked as the big assailant had been. He wore a hat with a wide brim pulled low over his face. He made no sound.

The man at the door was gasping now, not speaking, not pleading.

Rollison didn't speak. The man with the knife drew nearer, climbing two steps with stealthy movements. The man by the door pressed against the door-frame, as if he were trying to squeeze through it. He was making little ticking sounds as he breathed. Rollison couldn't see his face.

Then he saw the small man change his grip; he held the knife no longer as a dagger, but as if he were going to throw. That was the moment of deadly danger. Rollison, gun out of his pocket, pulled the door wide. The man suddenly pushed against it and fell in, sprawling, and the man with the knife seemed petrified.

Rollison fired.

The shot roared, the yellow flash was bright, the blade of the knife shattered. The assailant spun round. Rollison leapt forward, but as he went, knew that he was too late. The man who had come with the knife moved swift as a swooping hawk down the stairs. Rollison could shoot to wound, and meant to as he reached the head of the stairs.

The fleeing man reached the landing.

The door of the flat below opened, and a middle-aged man came bustling out, light streamed after him, the shadow of a woman as well as the man passed just behind the fugitive.

"Don't be absurd, Mary! A car back-fired—"

He broke off, breath rasping.

Rollison missed his golden chance, for by shooting now he might hit the neighbour. The fugitive bounded down the next flight of stairs. The street door was open. He went through, into the poorly lighted street.

The woman screamed.

The man, standing in his doorway as Rollison flew past him, made an ineffectual grab, crying: "Rollison, what—?"

Rollison felt the clutch of his hand, turned his head and flashed a smile. "I'll be back, it's all right." He went down to the street floor without a pause, but knew that he was too late, the fugitive had had time to run round either corner.

How had he come? By car, taxi, cycle, or on foot? If on foot, or if he had a car waiting round a corner—

Rollison reached the street.

Brakes suddenly squealed through the night, bringing the familiar moment of fearful apprehension that a crash was coming. A man shouted. Rollison saw two cars at the far end of Gresham Terrace, the Piccadilly end. A light at the corner showed everything plainly.

One "car" was a taxi, and two men were getting out of it and running towards the second car. And into this car a small man was climbing.

The car-driver was making the engine roar.

Rollison ran. "Stop him!" he shouted. "Stop him!"

Ahead was all confusion, although he believed he knew just what had happened. Behind came purpose, for a man was running as swiftly as he ran himself; a Yard man, Rollison felt sure. The car engine was still roaring. The car shot forward as the door slammed, there was a rending, squealing sound, men bellowed again and moved swiftly about in the yellow light. Then the little car won through and roared off towards Piccadilly, with two men running after it, oblivious of the futility. Another stood by the rear of the taxi, cursing with magnificent Cockney fluency.

Rollison slowed down.

The man running behind him drew level.

"What the devil's all this about?"

"Hallo," said Rollison, and had only to pause for breath, "I had visitors, and one of them ran away. Some friends of mine tried to stop him, but didn't quite make it, Sure you ought to reveal yourself?" he asked, earnestly. "Didn't Grice say—?"

"Never mind what Mr. Grice said!" The man gave himself away with hardly a thought. Undoubtedly his task was to watch the comings and goings at Rollison's flat, the sudden surge of excitement had drawn him out.

Rollison reached the taxi. The two men who had run so foolishly after the car were coming back, one of them with the respiratory rhythm of a grampus. A crowd had already gathered and was thickening, two policemen were making their unhurried way towards the scene.

The grampus, passing beneath a lamp, showed as an enormous man who walked with unexpected grace, wore a cloth cap that was too small for him, a folded choker and a white sweater. This was Bill Ebbutt. Rollison caught his eye and jerked his head towards number 22g and, at the moment when Grice's man was making himself known to a uniformed policeman, turned back towards his flat.

Grice's man saw him.

"Mr. Rollison! Please!"

"Oh, well," said Rollison, and tried to look pleasant. "Couldn't my statement wait?"

"We want *some* details," the Yard man said.

Ten minutes later Rollison walked towards the flat, with Ebbutt towering by his side at one shoulder and a smaller but equally tough East Ender, by name Charlie, at the other. A few curious passers-by followed them. The story to the police had been briefly told. Rollison forgot to mention the panic-stricken caller, simply made out that he had disturbed a burglar, who had fled. As the little man, in full flight, had reached his friend waiting in a small car, Bill Ebbutt and Charlie had arrived in a taxi. Ebbutt's mind was as sharp as any in London. He had tried to block the car's path and to catch the fugitive, but had failed at the cost of a badly dented wing and a wrenched bumper of the taxi. As the driver was undoubtedly a friend and crony, that would sort itself out with insurance connivance.

The police appeared to be satisfied, although the watching Yard man had surely seen Rory McGinn – if the man were really Rory.

The street door was open, two people from flats on the floors below Rollison's were conferring, and they regarded Rollison with no favour at all. He beamed upon them, and led the way upstairs.

He felt almost rested, no longer breathless, and much more secure. Now Bill Ebbutt and Charlie could wait outside, one at the foot of the fire-escape at the back, the other in front; and the big prisoner now on Jolly's bed would be given his chance to escape, and be followed. Rollison reminded himself that the trick was almost as old as the wooden horse of Troy; and no less effective because of its ancient lineage.

The flat door was open.

Rory McGinn – who else would it be but Rory? – was just picking himself up from the floor. He looked dazed, bewildered, frightened and foolish. He was rubbing his chin, where there was a sizeable swelling. Rollison took one look at him, and then went, sped by fresh alarm, into Jolly's room.

The bed was empty.

The big man had broken the cords at his wrists; there were the frayed ends. He had taken himself and his knuckle-duster and gone, and no doubt at all he had caused that swelling on Rory McGinn's chin. That was better than if he had used the knuckle-duster.

Ebbutt was in the doorway as Rollison turned.

"Bird flown?" he asked, sympathetically. "Everyfing alius 'appens at once, don't it? Never mind, Mr. Ar. Me an' Charlie'll put fings right. Ain't got much time, you know, if we've got to clout that six before Monday morning."

His grin showed broken and ill-shaped teeth, with many gold caps. He had a healthy look, though, in spite of his vast paunch. But there was something like scorn in his eyes when he looked at the American, who had also followed and was looking about him without comprehension.

"What six?" he asked, in a muffled voice.

"Forget it," said Rollison briskly, "it was just a figure of speech. We want to get the job finished before play starts on Monday, if we can. Are you Rory McGinn?"

The young American said: "Sure. Sure, that's me." He was a handsome and well-built, with curly chestnut hair and, now that the bewilderment was easing, attractive brown eyes. He looked massive enough to take on Ebbutt for five rounds; what had broken his spirit so completely?

"Oh, the ball game," he said, and shrugged – and so turned Ebbutt's scorn into fiery hostility. "If you'd gone to see my uncle instead of worrying about that damned game, this might never have happened."

"Mr. Ar," said Ebbutt, his breathing almost sulphurous, "is there anyfink more you want?"

"Soon, Bill," said Rollison. "Let's go and have a drink." He led the way into the big room, which Ebbutt knew well. He introduced Rory McGinn to Ebbutt and Charlie, and added: "You know where the beer is, Bill, help yourselves. Mr. McGinn, what will you have?"

"I guess I'll have a whisky-soda, thanks," said Rory McGinn. He was beginning to smile, as if the contrast between Ebbutt, Charlie and this flat and Rollison was showing up. "I didn't mean to be offensive. I just don't feel so good." He sat on the arm of a chair. "Only once before have I been scared like that, Mr. Rollison. I thought that guy was going to knife me. He was waiting outside my hotel, and followed me all the way."

Rollison was pouring whisky.

"Did you walk?"

"Sure. Why not? I left at eight o'clock, I had nothing else to do and was impatient to talk to you. It was a way of killing time. Then this guy came along. I tried to give him the brush-off, but couldn't find the way. When I reached the corner he showed the knife, and slashed at me. I just ran." Rory McGinn was suddenly pale again, as if talking about it brought that moment of danger back too vividly. "I guess I wasn't made for a hero, Mr. Rollison. I couldn't think of anything but getting here to see you. And—and I thought he'd kill me."

Rollison took a whisky-and-soda to Rory McGinn.

"It looked as if that was the idea. Here's to catching him."

"Thanks." McGinn gulped, and obviously made an effort to drive away the memory of terror. He drank. "Thanks a lot," he repeated, and actually forced a smile. "I thought everything was over when you went after the guy, but another one appeared from over there"—he pointed towards the door—"and before I knew what was happening, he'd put me down. Could that guy punch!"

"Not your lucky night," Rollison said, and was sharply conscious that he was stalling. "Have you had any message from your uncle?"

Rory McGinn said: "No." He turned pale again, drank deeply, then looked Rollison straight in the eye. "No," he repeated, "I'm afraid he's run into big trouble. I'm hoping you'll help to find him. He'd heard a lot about you, and hoped you would work for him."

"Do you know what he wanted?"

"No," said Rory McGinn, "he didn't confide in me. But I think he suspected he was being swindled by some jewel merchants, and wanted you to find out. I'm guessing, but it's a guess based on the little I do know. The guy's name was Fingleton, Jeremiah Fingleton. You ever heard of him?"

Chapter Eleven

The Bungalow

Rollison swung the wheel of his black Rolls-Bentley, and it purred over the narrow bridge across the Thames, near Heybridge. A few lights reflected on the water on either side. There was no sound, no other traffic about.

It was nearly midnight.

Rory McGinn, silent and subdued, sat by his side, Ebbutt behind. Rollison had simply told Rory that he had to go out, Rory could come and talk on the way if he wished.

Ebbutt's friend Charlie was in possession of the flat. The police had been there again and, probably on instructions from Grice, had been satisfied with another brief statement. They did not know about the man who had been a prisoner at the flat, but knew about Rory McGinn's part in the evening's sensation.

On the drive from London towards Heybridge, Rollison had found himself thinking as much of the fears of Rory McGinn as anything else. He kept seeing mental flashbacks of the little man with the knife. That man could use a knife expertly; the way he had twisted it in his fingers, turning it from a dagger to a throwing knife, had proved that. And he had followed Rory McGinn through London. A dozen times he had been close enough to leap and stab; or to hurl that knife into the American's heart.

He hadn't.

He could have killed Rory McGinn on the landing outside Rollison's flat, but had deliberately let his chance go by. The American might believe that the man had meant to murder him, and that Rollison had saved his life; but the evidence didn't say so. The evidence, if it could be called that, seemed to suggest that the little man with the knife had set out to terrify Rory ...

Or it could be taken to mean that the affair had been staged so as to get the door of the flat opened, distract Rollison's attention, and free the prisoner. If that were so, it could have been with or without Rory McGinn's connivance.

After the first whisky-and-soda at the flat, the American had become much calmer. He made it almost embarrassingly obvious that he was ashamed of his own fears; so, he seemed exceptionally honest.

"The guy scared me, Rollison, and I just couldn't do a thing about it. He seemed to hypnotise me. I would have started screaming next, I guess. And right now I'm still scared, although in a different way. I'd like to know what's happened to my uncle, and I'd like to know why that guy came after me the way he did. I won't be much good to myself or anyone else until I know." He had paused, to look into Rollison's eyes and to add with a faint puckering of his lips: "I'm told that you like living dangerously, but I'm not made that way."

Ebbutt had overheard this.

Afterwards, Ebbutt had said to Rollison: "You gotta say this for him, Mr. Ar—'e's honest abaht it."

Rollison was thinking of that, and of Rory McGinn's frankness as well as his story, as he drove over the narrow bridge.

The story hadn't helped much.

Rory was a vice-president of his uncle's steel corporation, and had charge of the European subsidiaries, with headquarters here in London. Connor McGinn had come for a vacation, as well as to look for jewels. Rory had been in Sheffield when his uncle had arrived in London, had travelled down that day, and reached the Miramar, only to find that Connor McGinn was out. He hadn't seen him at all.

Connor had talked freely to his nephew on the telephone; saying that he believed he was the victim of a big fraud, and wanted help, so was going to employ the Toff. That, Rory explained with a wry smile, was because he wanted a private eye who would take orders; unlike the police.

What Rory didn't appear to know was that two people were dead.

"I guess my uncle didn't mention this," Rory said suddenly. "He was anxious to spare my feelings, no doubt. But I'm very fond of a girl who works with the jewel merchants uncle was working with. And I'm worried about Bella," he added. "I've telephoned her at her apartment, and she doesn't answer. A man answered from her office, and sounded mighty mysterious. With my uncle missing, I guess I'm jumpy, but I can't help wondering if Bella's—"

"She's all right," Rollison said, "we're going to see her."

Rory McGinn seemed to become a different man; the car couldn't move fast enough for him.

Soon they were driving towards the Green, at Heybridge.

They reached a corner of a street of small houses.

A man stepped to the side of the road, and the headlights picked out Jolly.

A light shone at one window of the bungalow called Fingleton; just one light. It had been on for a long time, Jolly said. He hadn't seen the girl for at least two hours, and his last glimpse had been of her shadow against a blind. He didn't know whether she was in bed; he did know that the light was on in a sitting-room, because he had been close enough to see inside, before the blind had been pulled.

She might still be there.

Ebbutt and his men were now at other vantage points.

No one had come to the cottage; no one had left it. There it was, with one light burning, close to the River Thames. When the engine of the Rolls-Bentley was switched off, the men could hear the gentle lapping of the water at the end of the garden. There were no footsteps, no other sounds, only at one or two smaller houses were there lights, most of them dim and probably in homes where children slept.

"What are you going to do?" Rory McGinn asked. "If Bella wanted to find my uncle this morning, there's no reason to think that she knows where he is."

"The blind sometimes lead the lame," murmured Rollison. "I'm going—" He stopped.

A shadow appeared against the blind of the lighted room. It was the shadow of a woman. She stood upright for a moment, and must have been close to the window; her outline was sharp and clear, and strangely impressive. Rollison could picture the girl in all her beauty of face and figure.

She went away; presumably out of the room.

She left the light on.

Rollison moved forward, with no thought in his mind but knocking at the door and talking earnestly to Bella Daventry. Everything was so quiet, so normal, that there did not seem to be any chance that things could go wrong.

He was half-way across the road when another shadow appeared against the blind of a dimly lit room.

A man's.

Bella Daventry woke up with a start. At first she did not quite know where she was – just that she lay back in a chair, heavy-headed, heavy-eyed; but where? Then she saw the dark-brown carpet on which her stockinged feet rested. She had kicked off her shoes when she had sat down, pushed the cushion behind her back, and closed her eyes. She hadn't expected to fall asleep; she hadn't realised how near she was to exhaustion.

The bungalow, of course; Fingleton's bungalow – and no one was here.

No one had come.

She stood up quickly, as some do when waking in an unfamiliar place, slipped her feet into her shoes, and stood for a moment close to the window. She did not know that her silhouette showed so clearly. She rubbed her eyes and stretched, and then moved forward, going very quickly. Her mouth was dry and her eyes still very heavy.

She had taken three aspirins before sitting down, because her head had been aching so.

It still ached.

She wondered why Arthur Rowe, the other director of Fingleton's Limited, wasn't here. He should have been, for when in England he shared Jeremiah Fingleton's home. He always kept in the background, and she knew that there was good reason for that. But she had to see him now, had to tell him what was happening. As she thought of it, of crushed Jeremiah and knifed Paul, she shivered. It had been a nightmare day, and there must soon be an end to nightmare.

It was chilly, too.

She hadn't a thing to do, just had to wait. For the first time, she half wished that she had confided in Rollison. If it hadn't been for his icy manner at the Oval, she might have.

She went into the kitchen, filled the kettle, and lit the gas. The pop as it flared came loudly – and another sound, almost an echo, followed it, just at the door.

Bella swung round.

She had left the door open; and it was still open wide. She stared at it, mouth taut, lips parted with sudden fear.

There was no sound now. The gas was hissing, a few drops of water rolled down the aluminium side of the kettle and spluttered as the gas vaporised them.

"Who—who is there?" she asked, in a croaked voice.

There was no answer.

It had been imagination, of course, there was no one here; she had looked in every room of the bungalow before she had sat down. In spite of herself, she went into the little passage outside the kitchen – and then fear took terrifying possession of her.

There was a man – crouching.

"No!" she screamed. *"No!"*

The man leapt, with both hands outstretched.

Rollison was at the gate when he heard the scream. He was already moving fast, although there was no way of being sure that the man was in the bungalow unknown to the girl. Jolly was quite sure that no one had gone in or out, so the man must have been there when the girl had arrived. Yet something in the way his shadow had moved across the window had suggested stealth; furtiveness. So Rollison broke into a run.

He reached the gate – and the scream came.

Rollison raced along, calling: "Jolly!" The scream was loud enough to be heard outside. Ebbutt and the others would hear and close in, but they might not be in time; he might not be in time.

Two directors of Fingleton's were dead—

Rollison swung off the path and made for the window of the brightly lighted room, bent his elbow as he reached it, and smashed against the glass. It broke with a sharp crack.

He heard others running.

"No!" screamed the girl.

Rollison elbowed three long slivers of glass out of his way, put a leg through, scratched his left ear and his right hand, and almost fell into the room.

The screaming had stopped, there was gasping, scuffling sounds.

The door was wide open.

He reached it. There was a small, square hall, and several doors leading off it, as well as a narrow passage. There, the girl was fighting desperately against a little man who had a scarf in his hands, had twisted the scarf round her neck.

He knew that someone was coming.

As Rollison appeared, gun in hand, he took Bella Daventry's wrist and twisted.

She screamed with pain.

The little man pulled, then thrust her forward. Before Rollison had a chance to shoot without hitting the girl, he was behind her, using her as a shield.

"Get back," he ordered. "Get back, or I'll put a bullet in her, get back!" He had a gun in his right hand, and the muzzle pointed at Rollison. "Get back—"

He fired.

Rollison saw the stab of flame, and flung himself to one side. He felt nothing, then thudded against the wall. As he went, he was aware of a man rushing towards him, and then rushing past.

It was Rory McGinn.

Chapter Twelve

The Courage Of Rory McGinn

Rollison saw it all.

The helpless girl with the scarf round her neck, her terrified blue eyes, one arm held behind her and thrust cruelly upwards. The little man's head and the gun in his hand, smoking from the bullet which had just missed Rollison. And Rory McGinn.

McGinn was bellowing. It sounded just an animal gibberish. His handsome face was convulsed; Rollison saw it, being so close when the man rushed by. Rory didn't stop for a second, didn't hesitate, didn't seem to realise that the danger was waiting for him. The little man's gun was only a yard ahead; once the trigger was squeezed the bullet would bury itself in the American, he hadn't a chance of escaping it.

He yelled like a man demented.

It was just a single, lightning-like scene; over so quickly that it seemed hardly real.

Rollison saw him dose with the girl and strike at the gun. Had he struck it aside? There was a moment of wild confusion, with the girl sandwiched between the two men. Then Rollison recovered his balance, forgot the pain in his shoulder, and plunged forward.

He was too late; Rory had done all that was necessary.

The girl was leaning against the wall, her assailant was sliding down the other wall, eyes rolling, gun-arm hanging limply by his side. The gun was on the floor. Rory McGinn hit him again, although he was almost dead on his feet, and then turned towards the girl.

"She—she's all right," he muttered, and licked his lips. He was flushed, but his colour began to ebb. He narrowed his eyes and moistened his lips; unexpectedly, they began to quiver. "She—she is, isn't she?"

"Yes. Take it easy," Rollison said.

Then Jolly appeared from behind him, and the back door crashed in and two of Ebbutt's men arrived. They stared in astonishment at Rory McGinn, who moved away from Bella slowly, staggered into the kitchen, and dropped on to a wooden armchair. He buried his face in his hands; what little they could see of it was deathly pale.

"Wot the 'ell's the matter wiv 'im?" asked one of Ebbutt's men.

"He'll be all right. Slip him a spot of this, Jolly." Rollison handed Jolly his brandy flask, and Jolly began to pour brandy into a cup with as much aplomb as he would into a glass at the flat. He was the only one here who did not seem flustered or bewildered. Even the Toff watched Rory McGinn, trying to understand what made the man tick, and Ebbutt and two others, knowing they had been too long breaking in, were trying to pretend that they'd saved the world.

Bella Daventry was shivering.

Rollison took the scarf from her neck and then, to the surprise of all but Jolly, slid an arm beneath her knees and another round her shoulders, lifted her bodily and with great ease, and carried her into a bedroom leading off the hall.

He put her beneath the pink eiderdown, then punched pillows under her head, and turned to Jolly, who had come very quickly.

"A spot here, too."

"Yes, sir," said Jolly.

"Have one of the boys stay outside, to let us know if there's been any alarm," Rollison added.

"I've seen to that, sir, Mr. Ebbutt's gone himself." Jolly carried the brandy flask to Bella Daventry, and stood looking down at her.

In the struggle her dress had been torn at the shallow V at her neck. She was sun-tanned to the edge of that V; beyond it, her skin was milky-white. She was breathing deeply, still trembling, and clenching her hands and screwing up her eyes.

Rollison pulled up a chair, took her right hand, and began to stroke her forearm. It was nicely shaped, tanned on the outside, pale on the inside, but not so milky as the skin at her breast. A nice, smooth arm. Jolly made her take the brandy, and she swallowed a little; then Jolly went out, and Rollison begain to speak. He didn't say anything much, just told the girl gently that it was all right, she had nothing else to worry about, that no harm would come to her. She quietened. Obviously she was suffering from nervous tension and shock upon shock, and this last one had almost sent her round the bend. But she was no weakling, she wouldn't give in easily. Rollison sensed that, sensed also that she was already fighting to get back to normal. In half an hour he would know whether he ought to send for a doctor; now, there was a chance that it could be avoided.

He kept talking, and studying her.

She was very, very beautiful. She opened her eyes to look at him, and all the wonder of the sky was in the blue of her eyes. She was still quivering a little, but there was no longer tension in that nice forearm.

Jolly came in with two rubber hot-water bottles. With a barely audible by-your-leave, he put these beneath the eiderdown. The girl stared as he went out, turning at the door and bowing.

Rollison grinned.

Bella Daventry moistened her lips. "He—he's unbelievable!"

"That's the word for Jolly," Rollison said, "and for the rest of the world, sometimes. Think you'll be all right for five minutes? I want a chat with a bad man."

"The—the man who—?"

"The man whose right arm was hurt by a nephew of the fighting McGinns."

"Rory," she said. "Rory."

Rollison didn't speak at once, but watched her. She had that beauty which might well make heroes out of men who were usually full of fear. The way she said "Rory" suggested that the American mattered to her; as she mattered to him.

In her present mood, she might talk.

"Bella," Rollison said, "did you come here to meet Connor McGinn?"

She actually raised her head from the pillow.

"What on earth are you talking about? I came to see—" She broke off.

Rollison smiled, a very different smile from the one she had seen at the Oval. It had warmth and friendliness, which were meant to make her believe in his goodwill. "Here," it seemed to say, "is a man you can trust utterly and completely." She looked into his grey eyes and smiling face, and saw the invitation for her to tell the truth.

"I came to see Arthur Rowe," she said. "He—"

She paused.

"I know who you mean," said Rollison, showing no surprise at all. "Why did you expect to find him here?"

"When he's not abroad, he stays here."

"Why did you want to see him?"

She didn't answer at once. Her eyes were getting glassy, she needed rest—sleep and freedom from fear. He wondered if she were going to hide behind her need, and refuse to answer.

Then she spoke.

"I wanted—I wanted to tell him what had happened. About Paul and—" She stopped, and closed her eyes.

"And Jeremiah?"

She looked at him, helplessly. Her eyes were now much more glassy, and the change had come quickly. It was partly because she was back with her chief worry again, the main cause of her anxiety and her fears.

"Bella, what's frightening you? Why were you so scared at the Oval? Where does McGinn come into this?"

"I—I don't know."

"You know. And the sooner—"

"I don't know!" she cried.

"Listen, Bella, Jeremiah died. Paul went to kill him, didn't he? It wasn't done the way he planned, it was almost an accident, but he went to kill. Why?"

"I don't know!"

"You know something. What's the plot? Are you trying to fleece McGinn? Do you know where—?"

"I don't know anything," she sobbed, and turned her face away.

Rollison felt quite sure, then, that she wouldn't talk.

"I'll go and see the bad man," he said gently. "Take it easy."

He went out.

He didn't close the door.

Jolly, as if scenting his approach, appeared in the doorway of another lighted room. No one else had come, so the alarm had not been raised outside the bungalow. The quiet of the place and the murmur of the river outside had a soothing quality. Jolly was soothing, too.

"Mr. McGinn is feeling very much better, sir."

"Doctored by Jolly!"

"A little brandy, sir, and what one might call the psychological approach—I told him that but for him, Miss Daventry would almost certainly be dead. As, in fact, she might."

"Indubitably. How's the villain?"

"I'm not quite sure," said Jolly. "I felt sure that you would want to try to make him talk, and that the thing of importance is to find out where Mr. Connor McGinn is. I have asked Mr. Ebbutt to proceed along that line of inquiry. I don't know whether he's succeeded yet, sir. I've heard very little."

Jolly kept a completely straight face.

Rollison went into the lighted room. Rory McGinn wasn't there, but Ebbutt and one crony from Whitechapel were with the little man who had attacked Bella Daventry. He was stripped to the waist, and tied with his hands behind him to the foot of a single bed. His ribs showed against his pale skin. A sponge had been stuffed into his mouth. There was no sign of injury on his face or on his body, but the terror in his little, dark-blue eyes had to be seen to be believed.

Ebbutt was acting some kind of pantomime, using his fists. As Rollison went in, Ebbutt smashed his fists towards the prisoner's face, blow after blow shot out, but none touched, all stopped within an inch of the broken nose, the gaping lips, the sponge, the terrified eyes. Sweat stood out on the narrow forehead and ran down the pasty cheeks.

"All right, Bill," said Rollison. "That'll do."

Bill Ebbutt said: "Okay, but let me get at him in earnest if 'e don't talk."

Rollison pulled the sponge out of the prisoner's mouth; it expanded as if it were being blown up by a cycle pump; when he got it all out, it was almost as large as the little man's face.

He did not even look at Ebbutt.

"'E's lucky we didn't soak it in ammonia first," Ebbutt said fiercely, "make 'im firsty, that would. *Next* time—"

The little man mouthed animal sounds. Rollison gave him a few minutes grace, watching as he tried to work his lips and find his voice. Rory McGinn appeared at the doorway. His colour was back, and he was smiling; but he looked as if that took a great effort.

At last, Rollison said: "Now talk. Who sent you?"

The prisoner caught his breath, looked as if he would burst into tears, then began to talk; and words poured out. He lived here. He was Fingleton's and Arthur Rowe's manservant. Rowe was the boss – Rowe was an old lag, like him, and Rowe had told him that the girl would probably be coming. Rowe had ordered him to wait in the attic at the bungalow, to stay until he was sure no one else was coming to see Bella, and then—

"I wasn't going to kill her, guv'. Rowe just wanted to know if she'd talked to anyone, see. If you hadn't turned up I would have found aht and then left 'er okay." He let the words spill out, it was hard to believe that he had his wits about him enough to be lying. "Then I was to tell Rowe and get out, see. The girl wouldn't have been hurt. I swear it, don't let him—"

He looked with piteous entreaty from the Toff to Ebbutt.

Ebbutt gave another ferocious grin.

"Don't let him get at me!" the little man gasped.

"Just tell the truth and you'll be all right," said Rollison. "Where's Rowe now?"

"He's got a place in Soho, not far from the Garden, see." The shrill voice positively squeaked in the effort to sound convincing.

"That all you know?" asked Rollison.

"Yeh, yeh, everything."

Rollison looked at him for a long time, then shook his head and said: "Why were men born such liars? Have a go at him, Bill."

"Why, just what I've been waiting for." Ebbutt gave his broad grin, and actually spat on his hands. "When I've finished—"

"Keep him away!" sobbed the little man. "Keep him away! I'll tell you anything, anything."

Ebbutt rubbed his hands together with slippery menace.

Rollison stared into little eyes filled with terror; let the pause drag on, waited until Ebbutt went forward with fists clenched, and then rapped out: "Where's Connor McGinn?"

"He's with Rowe," gasped the little man. "Rowe planted a chauffeur on him, chap named Black Norris. Black took him to Soho."

"Why?" Rollison rapped into a pause.

"McGinn was on to us, knew we was dealing in hot stuff, in sparklers. If you want to save McGinn—" The voice was a hoarse whisper now.

Rory McGinn said brusquely: "Don't waste any time. Find out where they are, and—"

"Take it easy," Rollison said. "What's Rowe like to look at? Is there a photograph of him?"

"A big, square-faced cove," the little man burst out, "*and* he's a killer. He put Wrightson on to killing Jeremiah Fingleton. Jerry didn't know Rowe and Wrightson was playing it crooked. Paul did, but Paul—" The man was almost incoherent.

"What's that address?" cried Rory McGinn.

"You can't miss it, Fifty-nine Wilk Street, Soho, just off Greek Street. Side door. They're both there."

"Have you a key?"

"Yeh, yeh!" The man shook his leg, and coins and keys jingled in a pocket.

"Let's move." Rory was almost beside himself.

"We're on our way," Rollison said. "Jolly, look after Miss Daventry. Bill, have your buddy make sure this chap hasn't lied, and get all the extra dope he can. We'll clear the ropes for that six yet!" His smile flashed as he turned towards the door.

Outside, a third man from the East End said: "All quiet aht 'ere, Mr. Ar."

"Fine. Keep your eyes skinned." Rollison went swiftly down the gravel drive towards the car, which was parked off the road not far away. Soon, he was at the wheel, Rory McGinn by his side, Ebbutt leaning back in lordly grandeur in the rear.

"Rollison, I owe Connor McGinn everything I've got," said Rory in a tense voice. "We've got to get there in time."

"We'll get there," Rollison said, then added almost casually: "We could telephone Scotland Yard. The police might make it a cleaner job, and they'd be there an hour earlier."

"Never mind the police," Rory growled. "If you get there in time to save him, it'll be worth a thousand pounds to you. I'll guarantee it. Forget the police."

Rollison reached the open road, put his foot down, and sped towards London through Surrey's winding roads. He did not ask the obvious question aloud. Why was Rory McGinn ready to take a chance with his uncle's safety, so as to keep the police out of this?

The motive didn't matter now. Millionaire McGinn might be worth a fortune to Arthur Rowe while alive; he wasn't likely to be worth anything to him when dead.

So McGinn was probably alive.

As he drove on, Rollison found himself thinking of Bella, her hysterical refusal to talk, her fears and the way she had said "Rory".

They went on swiftly through the night.

Chapter Thirteen

Wilk Street

London slept.

Even Soho slept.

It was two o'clock. The most continental of the restaurants were closed. In one or two lights showed that the staff were still clearing up. No doors were open. A chill wind swept along the narrow streets. Now and again the quiet was broken by the snarl of a car engine. The engine of the Rolls-Bentley purred smoothly.

Rory McGinn sat stiffly by Rollison's side.

Rollison knew the heart of London as well as he knew the rabbit warren of the East End. He was familiar with short cuts, and could shame many a London cabby. The deserted streets encouraged speed. No policeman, walking steadily along trying the handles of the shops, took any notice of the speeding car. Lights turned green as if at a touch of Rollison's magic.

They turned into Greek Street, then reached Wilk Street. Rollison crossed this, and slid the car to a standstill just past the cross-roads. Before it had stopped, Rory McGinn had the door swinging open. There was a street-light at the corner, not bright, because Soho was a place of shadows and darkness, murder and mystery, a fabulous home for the stealthy figures of the half-world that was London's night life. In that dim light, Rollison saw Rory McGinn's face, its pallor and the set lips, which looked as if they would start quivering any moment.

He said: "McGinn, you can leave this to us. Be much better, we know the ropes, and—"

"To hell with that!"

Rollison said: "You've taken plenty tonight, and you won your red badge when you freed Bella Daventry. You don't have to be a hero again."

Rory McGinn glared.

"I'm coming."

"No," said Rollison, softly, insistently, "not this time, I can't take any chances." He saw the startled expression on the young American's face; then struck him swiftly and ruthlessly beneath the chin, at the point where it mattered.

Ebbutt turned, startled.

"Wot—?"

"Get him into the car, tie his wrists, make it slippy."

Ebbutt lifted Rory McGinn over his shoulder, grunted, and then pushed him into the car. The one street-light cast strange shadows. Rollison went softly to the doorway of Number 59. It was a side door, adjacent to the window of a small shop; the window wasn't lighted, but the street-light gleamed on tobacco and cigarette showcards.

Rollison used the little prisoner's key.

The door opened, without difficulty.

He stepped inside, then waited, getting used to the darkness, the smells and the sounds. There was a faint odour of garlic, mixed with cigar-smoke; that, and a sultry kind of silence. He seemed to stand there for a long time before Ebbutt joined him.

"He won't come rahnd for a bit, Mr. Ar. What's the idea?"

"He could crack up under pressure."

"Maybe." Ebbutt was non-committal. "We both going up at the same time?"

"I'll go first, and you give me a couple of minutes before following," Rollison said. "The little chap talked pretty smoothly. Rowe could have given him orders to squeal. There might be an ambush waiting for us."

Ebhutt sniffed.

"I'll use a torch," Rollison said. He took a pencil torch from his pocket, and the narrow beam shone straight at a narrow flight of stairs, on faded wallpaper and on linoleum. He went on, slowly. The darkness, the shadows, the silence, all plucked at his nerves. It had been quite a day. He was in a mood when he could do the wrong thing easily. He half expected a shot to come out of the darkness; everything that happened in this case seemed to come with explosive suddenness, giving no quarter.

He reached the top of the stairs.

There wasn't a sound, now. He shone the torch round, hearing his own heart thumping. Well, he was human. The light fell on doors, two ajar, one closed. He went to the open door and pushed it wider, then shone his torch round a small kitchen. The smell of garlic was stronger here; there was a smell of cooking, too, stewy and heavy. He backed out.

He heard a creaking sound behind him. Ebbutt's two minutes were up.

Then Ebbutt missed a step, gasped, fell with a crash. It shook the walls, and Rollison actually felt the floorboards quiver. He spun round – and struck the torch against the wall. The light went out as the bulb smashed.

His heart began to pound.

"*All right—Bill?*" He dared hardly whisper.

"*O-kay.*"

There were other sounds down the stairs, as Ebbutt picked himself up. Rollison waited for the grampus-like breathing, but it didn't come. His heart steadied, and with it came greater relief than he had known for a long time. No one had called out in alarm, there had been no sounds apart from Ebbutt's fall. If Rowe or Black Norris were lying in wait, they would have moved by now.

The stairs creaked.

"Take it easy," Rollison whispered. Then he decided that he dared risk a light. His relief had ebbed a little, a different kind of anxiety took its place. Would McGinn be here if there were no guard?

He reached a door next to the kitchen. A beam of light shot out from the stairs; Ebbutt carried a torch, so the landing light wasn't necessary.

Rollison was cautious, although the need for caution was less urgent. He turned the handle of the door, and pushed. The door didn't open. He dropped a hand to his pocket for his knife, saying: "Shine it on the keyhole, Bill."

The torch moved.

Rollison opened the knife to the skeleton-key blade. This lock could have been picked with a hairpin, it was hardly worth calling a lock; yet someone or thing who mattered lay beyond it. He heard the lock click back. He took the skeleton key out, snapped the blade into position, then tried the door again.

It opened.

"Careful," he breathed.

The door did not creak. When it was open a foot, he stood with his head just inside the room, ears strained to catch any sound. At first, he heard none, but soon he detected the sound of soft, even breathing.

But surely no one would have slept through the din of Ebbutt's fall.

Rollison groped for the light switch, found it, and pressed it down. There was Connor McGinn.

The American lay on a single bed, a mountainous heap. He lay on his back with his hands folded across his stomach, the fingers interlaced. The bright light shone just above his face, but he didn't move an eyelid. He had rather a pleasant face, with a big, prominent nose and sensitive lips; and it would be easy to believe that his lips were curved in a smile. He was fully clad, even to his gleaming brown shoes, but the ten-gallon hat was on top of one of the iron posts of the bed.

"So they drugged him," Rollison said, and glanced round. "And we've got him, Bill, and—"

The man holding the torch wasn't Ebbutt.

It was the big brute: Black Norris.

Black Norris was only a couple of feet away from Rollison. He held the torch in his left hand, and the brass knuckle-duster was on his right. His fist was clenched and raised. He grinned, as if he had never enjoyed anything so much as Rollison's stupefaction.

Rollison might have been struck with paralysis; even his facial muscles were stiff.

"So you thought your dear old pal slipped," sneered the big man. "So he did, Toff, after I'd cracked his skull. He'll come round some other time—maybe. As for you—I told you what I was going to do to you, didn't I? And I warned you to keep your nose out of other people's business. Know how I'm going to start? I'm going to push that nose right into your face, see."

He drew his mailed fist back.

Here was a man with the strength to kill him, the strength and the will to smash Rollison's face into a shapeless, bloody mess. The strength, the will and the weapon. And Black Norris grinned as if he wanted nothing better. He held that knuckle-duster like a sword of Damocles, savouring his triumph to the full.

Then he drove the mailed fist forward with awful strength.

Rollison swayed from the hips. The knuckle-duster tore a piece of skin off his ear, and sharp pain stabbed. He didn't back, or kick, or punch. He used the split second while the man was off his balance, shot both hands up, gripped the powerful wrist and huge forearm. He twisted, so that Black Norris was almost helpless and couldn't get his other arm up.

The muscles were like slippery steel as the man twisted and turned, trying to free himself, knowing exactly what Rollison was striving to do.

Every muscle, every nerve in Rollison's body was strained to this supreme effort; to break the big man's arm. Break it, and the knuckle-duster might as well be made of putty. Break it, and he would live without hideous disfigurement. Break it, and he would get Connor McGinn out of here, safe in his drugged unconsciousness.

Rollison had the proper hold.

He forced the arm up, up, up. He felt the muscles and the sinews moving, tightening, flexing, exerting awful effort. He felt the great shoulders go slowly backwards, but slowly, with a giant's will-power, Black Norris managed to get his other arm into use. A hand fluttered at first at Rollison's throat, then fingers pressed and prodded, then worked their way round until they almost spanned the neck. Pressure increased against Rollison's wind-pipe. Now it was one or the other, touch and go, with the odds heavily against him.

Both hands straining every sinew, he thrust savagely upwards. Black Norris's arm was rigid like an iron pipe; or an unbending steel tube. An inch, half an inch farther, and the bone would crack just above the elbow.

Fingers were tight at his own throat, a thumb was pressing against his wind-pipe. He could feel pressure everywhere; his eyes seemed to force their ways against their lids. The weight of the blood in his ears was agonising. His heart beat in swift, laboured, pounding thuds. He could hardly breathe because of that choking pressure. Win or lose, it wouldn't be long now.

He heard a different sound; gasping breath; grampus-like breathing. *Ebbutt?* His heart expanded with fierce hope. Then he realised that it wasn't Ebbutt, but the big man fighting for breath, fighting just as desperately as Rollison.

Something wet dropped on to Rollison's hands; sweat from the big man's forehead.

Up, up, up, forcing against that rigid arm, that arm which could not bend or swivel up any farther, which had to stay there, come down, or—crack.

Crack!

It went up, limp, helpless, broken.

An awful cry escaped Black Norris's lips. It reeked with more than pain; it held agony of the body and of the mind. He knew that he had lost. Every nerve and muscle in his great body had been strained to win, and he had lost. There was just the one howl, high-pitched, bestial – and then gasping, grunting quiet.

Rollison backed away.

He felt his knees bend under him. Sweat poured down his face and his body. He swayed helplessly, with no idea which direction he was moving. His head was going round and round, round and round, and there were great swirling mists in the room, mists which took on the shape of the big man's grinning face.

He banged into something hard.

He sprawled sideways, and collapsed across a soft and yielding mass. He lay still. His ear was pressed tightly against that mass, and he could hear a strange thumping sound. If his heart pounded like that, it would give out.

He knew that he was nearly unconscious.

He couldn't understand this dynamo thudding in his ear.

He tried to move, but couldn't. He flopped, and lay still. He began to think of the big man whose armoured fist was helpless now, but who still had one good arm and physical strength given to few. He would still want to kill. Once he came round, he would be thirsting for revenge. If he came again, he would win; Rollison had no strength left.

Suddenly, there came a sound of a whistle, and thudding. His heart began to pound again, somehow he forced himself to his feet. The door was open. Black Norris had gone, and the din came from the stairs.

Chapter Fourteen

Frustrating For Grice

The thudding continued after the shouting had stopped. Then that slackened and faded, and for a while there was quiet. Rustling sounds came from some way off, but did not disturb the hush of the room. Rollison was upright, and looking about him. He had the sense to realise that he had been lying across Connor McGinn, whose great body hadn't moved, whose expression hadn't changed.

He managed to get out a handkerchief to wipe his face and forehead. It was a wet rag in a moment. He pushed it back into his pocket.

Jolly had his flask.

He took a step towards the open door, then heard sharper sounds, as of a man walking on the stairs. Next moment, a whistle blew; a police whistle, of course, that's what he had heard the first time. He went slowly towards the door with great deliberation, determined to be upright when he reached it. He heard men running outside, then hurrying up the stairs. He did not know that his shadow was thrown out into the landing, and that men watched, warily.

He staggered from the room.

Three policemen, each with truncheon drawn, were waiting for him. He saw them as if he were seeing treble. He looked from one to the other, slowly, blinking, grinning foolishly.

"Be fair," he admonished. "Three to one won't do. Not British. Play the game. Straight bat and all that. What'sh the—what'sh the latest score. And ide—"

He swayed.

A policeman, sensing true collapse, moved swiftly and held him up. But he hadn't really lost consciousness, and something brought him sharply and painfully back to reality. He fought against the constable's restraining hold, and shouted in a voice that was suddenly loud and powerful. "Ebbutt! Where's Ebbutt? Bill!"

"We found a man at the foot of the stairs, sir," the policeman said, firmly. "Knocked out, but not hurt badly. Now stop shouting and keep still, will you?" He became brusque.

"Not hurt badly?" echoed Rollison. "Good old Bill. Skull of stainless steel. You haven't a spot by you, have you? ... Pity ... Because in there, there's a cause for international tension. Ask Grice. Mr. Grice. Super—Super—Super Grice to you."

"He means *Superintendent* Grice," a policeman said, as if in horror.

Grice, who liked a double bed, heard the telephone bell ring, and felt his wife's breath falling gently on to his arm, which was under her shoulder. The bell kept ringing. He shifted his position as gently as he could, but felt her start. So she was awake.

"All ri'," he muttered. "Telephone."

"What, dear?"

"Telephone."

"It's still dark. Not morning yet."

"No. Telephone." Grice pulled his arm free, sat up, and snatched the hand-piece off the receiver. "Hallo?" he growled, half hoping that by being vicious he would be spared a journey to the Yard. "Eh? ... What? ... *Who?*"

Two minutes later, quite wide awake, he said quietly: "You settle down, darling, no need to wake up. I've got to nip over to the Yard."

He was at the Yard at precisely four o'clock ...

He learned that a patrol officer in Soho had first found Rory McGinn unconscious in Rollison's car; then found a door open, gone into the passage beyond and almost fallen over an unconscious man, now known to be Ebbutt. Then another man had rushed out, and got away with the help of two others who hadn't been seen until too late.

Finally, Rollison had been found ...

Grice was at the Gresham Terrace flat at half-past five. By then, Rollison was back, and Jolly was there and in full charge. Grice, knowing him well, could tell that Jolly was almost asleep on his feet, for his brown eyes were red- rimmed and glassy, and he had to form his words with excessive care. But strangers would have seen only a rather comical, pompous and pedantic little man.

"I am sorry, Mr. Grice, I know no more than that. Mr. Rollison made this little man talk at Heybridge, and went rushing to London—to Soho. Mr. Rory McGinn was with him. Do I understand you to say that Mr. *Connor* McGinn has been found?"

"Yes, Rollison found him, but—"

"He's quite incapable of rational comment now, sir," Jolly said. "But of course, you—ah—you realise that yourself, don't you?" He closed his weary eyes for a moment, then opened them very wide, owlishly. "I warmly appreciate the fact that he was brought home. Do I understand that Mr. Connor McGinn is—unhurt?"

Grice said: "So you don't know."

"I don't know a thing, sir. Did you catch anyone besides Mr. McGinn and Mr. Rollison?"

"We found Rory McGinn in Rollison's car," said Grice. He gave the impression that he didn't quite know what to say or how to handle this situation. "I'll be round in the morning early, Jolly. Make sure that the Boss doesn't try to leave. We want the whole truth, this time."

"Mr. Rollison's usually a reliable witness, sir," said Jolly, and for the moment was almost bland.

Grice rubbed his chin very slowly, then gave a grudging smile.

"I see. Now what's this about Miss Daventry?"

"Naturally I took it for granted that Mr. Rollison would want her to be made comfortable and secure for the night, sir, and as we have a spare room, I brought her here. She is asleep. Late though it was, I had Mr. Rollison's doctor to see her, and he gave her a sedative. I should be very reluctant indeed to wake her now."

"Don't be reluctant when I come next time," growled Grice. "Anything else?"

"There is one thing that Mr. Rollison doesn't know about," Jolly said. "I had a telephone call soon after I got back here. A man said that Mr. Connor McGinn would be found in a house in Wilk Street, Soho."

"Who was it?" Grice demanded.

"The man didn't give his name," Jolly said regretfully. "Could it be that someone is on the point of cracking?"

"I don't know," Grice admitted, scowling.

Grice left a man in the street, then went to the Yard and made arrangements for a general call to go out if Bella Daventry left Rollison's flat.

For the second time within twelve hours, Bella Daventry woke up in a strange room. Only this time she was not in an armchair, and she didn't feel stiff. She did feel frightened. Her nerves seemed to scream as she lay peering about her. It was morning, because the sun shone through a corner of the window of the small room. A clock ticked softly, and after the first shock of waking and the discovery that she was alone, she looked at the clock.

It was half-past eleven.

She struggled up on her soft pillow, and realised then how comfortable it was, how superbly soft and springy the bed was. It was a single, and opposite the foot was a small but exquisite dressing-table, the centre and the wing mirrors gilded. This seemed a woman's room. On the dressing-table were the little oddments of *toilette*; and brushes, combs – there was her ring, her only valuable ring, on a small stand.

She looked round more boldly.

Her clothes were neatly folded by the side of her bed. The stockings were draped over the back of the chair, and she could tell from here that they were riddled with ladders. That was a momentary important grief, before she began to remember clearly.

The bungalow; the little man; Rollison; Rory McGinn, who had flung her from the murderous little man; and then Rollison again; a different being, with his gentle voice and soothing hand and wholly captivating smile. She had trusted him then, and she believed she could trust him now.

And Jolly—

There was a tap at the door. She started, and stared; the tap was repeated. The mirror told her that she was wearing only a slip, and one strap had fallen off her shoulder. She looked about, almost desperately, felt silly and foolishly prudish – and then saw a fluffy angora wool bed-jacket, a lovely pink shade, on a chair by the side of the bed. She draped this round her shoulders quickly.

"Come in!"

The door opened, and Jolly appeared – a smiling Jolly with a twinkle in his eyes.

"Good morning, madam. I hope you slept well."

"Yes, I—yes, thanks!— But where—where am I?"

"Mr. Rollison is happy to be able to extend to you the hospitality of his apartment, madam," said Jolly, "and presents his compliments and hopes that you would like some tea."

"Oh, yes, please!"

"Very good, madam," said Jolly. "May I draw the curtains?"

"Er—oh, yes,"

He went to the window, like a black-clad automaton, drew the curtains gravely, turned and bowed, and went out.

Bella looked about her again. This was certainly a woman's room, and she knew that Rollison was a bachelor. It was small but delightful. And the bed was so comfortable—

She discovered that she wasn't frightened as she had been. The sight of Jolly and the comfort of the room had somehow eased her fears. She could lean back and relax.

Then there was another tap at the door.

"Come in."

Rollison pushed the door open with his foot, and came in carrying a tea-tray on one hand.

Tall and absurdly handsome, wearing a magnificent dressing-gown of navy blue silk, freshly shaved, dark hair glistening and boasting its few strands of grey, mobile lips set in a smile, his grey eyes were laughing as if at the best joke in the world. There was a neat patch of sticking-plaster on the side of his chin, another on his right ear. He put the tray on the bedside table, pulled up a chair, and then, without a word or hint of what he was going to do, bent over her and kissed her, full on her soft lips.

He drew back.

"Hallo," he said.

Something in his expression and the tone of his voice made her want to laugh. Her eyes showed it. He took both of her hands and leaned over her, looking down as if intent on finding the slightest flaw.

His smile became gradually more sober.

"Perfect," he said. "One day I really shall."

"You'll really do what?"

"Kiss you properly, because one should experience everything." He dropped into the chair and poured tea.

"You're looking a hundred times better. I'm told that I am too." He handed her a cup, and went on: "But you don't know, do you? All's well! Well, most of it. We found Connor McGinn. Nephew Rory has been on the telephone three times this morning, too make sure that we aren't ill-treating you. You've made quite a hit with Rory McGinn."

She stopped smiling.

"Do you say you *found* his uncle?"

"Safe, drugged, fatuous. I don't really know what he's like when he's conscious, do you?"

"I've only spoken to him over the telephone," she said. She sipped her tea, and watched Rollison closely. It was obvious that he was still amused, but he might be pretending. She was much less composed than she had been.

"Did he—?" She broke off.

"Bella," said Rollison, "yesterday afternoon at the Oval, we had a little chat. You said that you hoped you didn't know what had happened to Connor McGinn. What did you mean?"

She hesitated, and then said: "He had some jewels belonging to— belonging to my firm. They'd been left at the hotel, on approval. I wasn't sure whether he could be trusted. I hoped he hadn't run off with them, but rather thought he might have done just that."

There was something brave about her lie.

"Drink your tea while it's hot. Why should he?"

"I don't know." She was very ill-at-ease, as if realising that Rollison wasn't deceived. "He—he sounded a tremendous bluffer on the telephone. Paul—Paul Wrightson had taken the jewels to the hotel." She stopped again, and for a moment her eyes closed, as if she were trying to shut out a vision. Then she opened them again, and it was easy for Rollison to believe that she was calling on all the courage she had. "I thought that he might have run off with them, or even been attacked and robbed. That would have ruined the firm, so—I hoped I was wrong."

Rollison said mildly: "I see. And what about insurance?"

"They weren't insured," said Bella Daventry. She put her tea down, as if she couldn't drink another drop. "I know they should have been. Paul—Paul was—wasn't himself. He—" She paused, very pale again. "Did you tell the police I killed—I mean, that I was there when he died?"

Rollison said mildly: "They found out, Bella, but that needn't worry you, because I saw what happened. You aren't in danger about that, and it wasn't your fault, the horror will fade. But why did Paul go to lull Jeremiah? Did you know that's what he'd gone to do?"

She didn't answer.

"Did you?" Rollison insisted softly.

Chapter Fifteen

Day Of "Rest"

Bella didn't answer, didn't look at Rollison. He waited, patiently, admiring her beauty, finding it easy to believe in her honesty. Grice would sneer about Sir Galahadding, but let Grice sneer.

She looked up, her gaze disconcertingly direct.

"I was afraid so," she said. "Paul—Paul quarrelled with Jerry, yesterday morning. There was a lot of wild talk. Arthur—Arthur Rowe calmed them down. But I saw what happened outside the Oval. Paul—Paul tried to knock Jerry over, but lost his nerve. The van did it for him."

How her eyes showed the shocked horror of all that.

"Do you know why they went to the Oval? Why it happened there?"

"No," Bella said. "They're all cricket crazy, always at the Oval, *always.*"

"So it didn't seem strange that it should happen there."

"No," Bella agreed. "I saw Jerry first, and wasn't a bit surprised. Then Paul—" She broke off.

Rollison did not let her brood.

"You had to challenge Paul, and you did," he said. "Why was he so scared? What was his quarrel with Fingleton about?"

She didn't answer.

"Rowe?" asked Rollison.

Her eyes flashed. "No! Arthur was always calming them down. Paul—Paul bought some stolen jewels, Jerry said he knew they were stolen."

"Did he?"

"I—I think so," he said. "He was usually hard up, someone was always after him for money."

"But why should he want to kill?"

This time, she didn't try to evade the question. She was much calmer, and spoke as if she knew that she could trust Rollison.

"Because Jerry said he would go to the police."

"Would he?"

"He might have done."

"What did Rowe say about it?"

"He's always—sympathetic," Bella said, and if it hadn't been apparent before, it was now clear that she was deeply attached to the missing Arthur Rowe—who employed men like Black Norris if the little crook had told the truth, and who had not hesitated to have her terrified; perhaps was ready to have her killed.

"In what way sympathetic?" Rollison asked.

"He said he was sure that Paul had slipped up, and wouldn't do that again. When he left, they—they *seemed* friendly."

"Do you know where he is?"

"No." That came quickly. "But I never trusted Lemaitre. Nor did Arthur."

"Lemaitre?"

"The man at Heybridge."

"Oh, I see." She seemed deliberately blind to Arthur Rowe's possible faults, "Bella, let's try to get it all sorted out," Rollison went on almost casually. "Why did you want to see McGinn? Why did you come to see me? Why did you run away?"

Each question fell like pebbles into a pool, rippling in widening circles, striking the girl with increasing force. Yet she didn't look away from him.

"I was—afraid—that Paul was going to swindle Mr. McGinn."

"How?"

"I don't know. I'd heard him say that McGinn might be the answer to all his prayers. And I—I knew Rory. Paul had met Rory at some club, he introduced us. I didn't—I didn't like the thought that Rory or his uncle would be cheated. I went to warn McGinn, and—and saw you. If you'd behaved differently—"

"Don't rub it in," pleaded Rollison. "Why not warn Rory?"

"I did. He said I was crazy, and laughed it off."

"Did he?" murmured Rollison, then paused, then went on quickly: "All right, Bella, people do hate thinking badly of their friends. Why did you run away from me? Why pack clothes and rush down to Heybridge? You knew I'd seen the killing at Paul's flat, there was no need to panic."

She said slowly: "But I did panic. I'd seen two—two of my best friends die. And I was terrified. I had just one idea, to see Arthur, I knew he'd tell me the right thing to do. But—he couldn't get there."

"To Heybridge?"

"Yes."

"Did he know you were going."

"Yes. He telephoned me, we were to meet—" She broke off, and dread came back to her eyes.

Rollison didn't speak. Her thoughts were clear enough, she had seen the implications; that Rowe had planned the attack on her.

"No!" she exclaimed. "He wouldn't do it, there was no reason why he should!"

"We don't know who was so anxious to kill you, or who Lemaitre works for," Rollison said. "We'll find out. Was there any other urgent reason for seeing Arthur Rowe?"

She didn't answer.

"You know." said Rollison, "I don't have to tell the police all I find out. There's no way that they can make me tell. If Arthur Rowe's the man you think he is, I won't do anything to injure him."

He smiled.

Obviously, he'd struck the right note,

"Arthur had been in prison, for jewel robbery, years ago," she said abruptly. "I knew that. He couldn't come into the open, but he was invaluable to the firm. I had to find out if he knew that Paul was buying stolen jewels, if he had anything to do with—with planning to swindle McGinn. Until I knew, I couldn't tell you a thing."

"And supposing he had known all about it?" asked Rollison.

"I'd have given him a chance to escape, then told the police," she said simply. "What else could I have done?"

He knew that he might be a fool; but he believed her.

If there were a plot on foot against McGinn, she could hamper it badly, perhaps ruin its chances of success.

Was that why she had been so nearly killed?

Rollison didn't force more questions about Rowe, but moved away, and poured out more tea. He took cigarettes from his dressing-gown pocket and held them out.

"No, thanks."

"Not so early in the morning?"

"I don't smoke at all."

"Wise girl." Rollison sipped tea, lit a cigarette, and looked at her through the cloud of grey smoke. "Was Rowe really the mainspring of the business?"

"Well, yes, I suppose so," she agreed. "He always kept in the background. Paul did the buying, Jerry the selling, and I tried to tie up all the ends. I usually dealt with Arthur." She stopped; sensing the question in Rollison's grey eyes. "He'd stolen jewels years ago, in South Africa. He was truthful enough about it. We all knew. It was robbery with violence, although he—he didn't use violence himself, his accomplice did. He came out of prison seven years ago. I—I knew him before he was caught. He was a friend of my mother, we used to live in Natal. I think—"

Soon she was talking because she wanted to. All this had been bottled up for years, and flooded out now.

Her parents had been ill-matched; a long-suffering mother, a harsh and sometimes brutal father—brutal to his wife, but not to his daughter. Arthur Rowe, a friend first of the family, had been the one bright spot, someone to like, to offer help and understanding. But:

"There was never anything between him and mother," Bella Daventry said. "They weren't living together." She broke off, but did not keep silent for long. Her chin went up. "Then my mother died, and my father died soon afterwards. Arthur became a kind of unofficial uncle and father combined. I was only twelve at the time. He didn't mind what he did to help me. Sometimes I think that he began to steal so as to give me the best education he could. It wasn't until I was fifteen that he was arrested, and I found out what he'd done."

"I'd like to meet your Arthur Rowe," Rollison said, and nothing could have pleased her more. "And I'd like to get the truth out of Lemaitre, too. Ever heard of a man named Norris—called Black Norris?"

Bella looked blank.

"No."

"Forget it. Forget everything and don't worry." Rollison moved towards the door. "Now, take it easy. The bathroom is the door on the right outside, it's free for as long as you need it. Breakfast whenever you say—Jolly will look in. You're going to take it easy today."

"What are you going to do?" asked Bella.

He grinned.

"I'm going to think, and then try to think some more. Any idea who Paul bought these stolen jewels from?"

"No."

"Care to guess?"

"I can't guess."

"Any idea at all where I might find Arthur Rowe?"

"Mr. Rollison," Bella said, quite clearly. "If I had, I'd tell you. I just don't know."

"All right, Bella *mia,*" said the Toff, and beamed, and went out.

She looked at the door. He seemed to have taken something of the brightness out of the room, although it remained lovely, and the sun still shone through one corner.

After a while she pushed back the bedclothes and got out of bed.

Rollison fingered the little patch at his chin when he left Bella, and wandered, as if absently, into the kitchen. There Jolly was cooking bacon and eggs; perfect timing, although possibly Jolly's ear had been at the keyhole for a while. Toast was already in a rack, a golden brown, two trays were laid, a kettle was singing, fat was bubbling, and Jolly was spooning it over the eggs, to give them a soft, filmy coat.

"And what did you make of her story?" asked Rollison, still absently.

"I beg your pardon, sir?" Jolly was bland.

Rollison grinned.

"All right. She's a nice girl. I believe her. I wonder whether Grice will. I wonder whether her Arthur Rowe and Black Norris could be one and the same." He scowled. "I hope not." He sniffed. "Yes, I am hungry. What did you find in the pockets of the little man who told us where to find McGinn?"

"Very little, sir," said Jolly. "He had nothing in his clothes to help identification, but he was so frightened that he readily gave his name and home address. He has the unusual name of Lemaitre, and his home is at Five Poll Court, not very far from Mr. Ebbutt's establishment. But he lives in at Heybridge, as manservant to Mr. Jeremiah Fingleton and to Mr. Arthur Rowe, when Rowe is in England. He travels a lot." Jolly lifted eggs out of the pan expertly, and placed them on a large plate. "Lemaitre has worked for Rowe on and off for some years. At one time in South Africa they were— ah—partners in crime. He says that he knew nothing about these current incidents until Rowe gave him those orders today. Just one unexpected piece of information will be of particular interest to you, I think."

"Really? What?"

"Excuse me one moment, sir." Jolly placed the slice in the pan, then slid a hand beneath his white carpenter's apron, and drew it out with a flourish.

He handed Rollison an Oval score-card.

This was crumpled and soiled, had the corner of a heel imprint on it, and was partly filled in with ball-point ink in a spidery writing.

Even names printed on the card were misspelt where Lemaitre had filled in details.

The fact that he had been at the Oval jolted Rollison sharply.

Black Norris had also been there. And like Norris, Lemaitre had filled in the score up to the fall of Hassett's wicket, after lunch.

"So presumably they left at the same time," said Rollison, very thoughtfully. "About three o'clock."

"So it appears, sir."

Rollison nodded, then looked at crisp bacon, two eggs, bread fried to a crisp dark brown, and two halves of a large tomato. Jolly waved a hand something like a prima donna imploring a generous audience to include the orchestra leader or her pianist in its applause.

"Yes, I'll eat it while It's hot," the Toff promised. "Take Miss Daventry's in."

"Very good, sir." Jolly soon vanished.

Half an hour later, Rollison telephoned Bill Ebbutt and learned from his earnest wife that he was having breakfast in bed and had a lump on his head as big as a duck's egg. The Toff promised to look in during the day, rang off, then tapped at the spare-room door, and when invited, put his head round it.

Bella looked what she was; beautiful.

"I really can't stay here all day," she said.

"Get up any time you like, but the longer you rest the better you'll feel. Is Arthur Rowe a cricket fan, or just an Ovalite?"

"He does go to Lord's sometimes, but usually to the Oval."

"Was he there yesterday?"

"Yes. He said he was going, anyhow. I—" Her eyes rounded, her arms, resting on the bedspread, stiffened suddenly. "Oh, *no*," she breathed.

"No what?"

"Jerry wasn't going to him, was he? He hadn't told Jerry to meet him there."

She hated to think of what this might imply: that Jeremiah Fingleton had been summoned to his death by her beloved Arthur Rowe.

The amazing thing, Rollison realised, was that her fears were all for Rowe, none for herself. But a man had gone to kill her. Someone, probably Rowe, wanted her dead.

Rollison was scared for her.

Half an hour later, Grice arrived. Rollison, in his dressing-gown, greeted him, amiably. Grice, brown-clad, brown-faced, eyes very bright and looking as if they would miss nothing, came in briskly, nodded to Jolly, and had a strong "no nonsense" air.

"Hi, Bill," Rollison said. "How are the McGinns?"

"Rory's got a stiff neck, thanks mostly to you, and his uncle's a bit under the weather," said Grice, "but they're all right. The old boy seems to want to make you a millionaire. I'd make you a pauper if I had my way."

"Bitter, Bill, bitter!"

"So I should be. I've had a better look at this job now, and I don't like your capers. You ought to have reported everything about the Wrightson business at once, and when you heard where McGinn was, last night, you should have called us. If you'd arrived too late, McGinn might have been murdered."

"But he wasn't."

"No thanks to you."

"Unjust, ungrateful and unstrung," breathed Rollison brightly. "Someone has been angry with you, I can see. Let me conjure up visions. American Embassy, anxious for the safety of dear Millionaire McGinn, has a V.I.P. contact Home Secretary early on Sunday morning. That's enough to put Home Sec. in a sultry mood for the week. Home Sec. gets Assistant Commissioner out of bed, and breathes hell and damnation. A.G. stretches out for a hatchet and Grice's neck. My dear chap—"

Grice had the grace to grin.

"You're not far wrong, at that! But you shouldn't have taken the chance. You weren't to know that he would be drugged."

"No. Just hoped. I couldn't imagine Millionaire McGinn much use to anyone when dead, but all alive-o made him a fish of a different odour. So I hoped. What's Millionaire McGinn's story?"

"The kind we've often heard before," said Grice, with a grimace. "He couldn't get you to help him, knew that Rory was fond of the Daventry girl, and didn't want to consult us. After arranging to call on you, he had a telephone call from Rory, and that made him too late. So he went to see Paul Wrightson, but got nowhere. Then he went to see Fingleton, who was out. He was driving his own car— one of his London office cars, that is. He got lost, so he telephoned the office for a chauffeur."

"Oh, did he?" said Rollison, softly.

"What's on your mind?"

"Forget it."

Grice glowered.

"One of these days I'll remember everything against you. He finally went to see Paul Wrightson again, got no answer, went back to the hotel car park, and was slugged by his chauffeur. You need not inquire at the London office— I'll see to that."

"Granted," said the Toff. "How is he, anyway?"

"He'll be under the weather today, that's all."

"How does he get on with his nephew, do you know?"

"No. Why?"

"Rory McGinn didn't want me to tell the police anything."

"What?"

"Fact."

"Know why?"

"No. I just guess, and that wouldn't be any good for a conscientious copper, would it? Rory might be nervous about the possibility that his uncle was buying stolen gems. I don't know. Or else that his girlfriend was mixed up with a gang of crooks."

Grice said: "They're just angles. Anything to use for evidence, or are you trying to sort this one out by sticking pins in wherever it might hurt?"

"No evidence. Found Arthur Rowe?"

"No. Do you know where he is?"

"No," said Rollison. "Nor does Bella Daventry."

"I'm just going to find that out," Grice said.

He sent for a sergeant, who was outside, and questioned Bella for twenty minutes. Rollison did not know what line he took. Grice seemed dissatisfied when he came out of her room. He sent the sergeant off, then said to Rollison: "She's a looker, but she might also be a liar. She won't breathe a word against Rowe."

"That's not news," Rollison said.

"Maybe not. Be careful on this job, Rolly."

"Yes, Bill." Rollison sounded humble. "Found any jools?" he asked, almost an afterthought.

"No. McGinn hadn't got them with him, but hasn't produced them yet. They hadn't got around to robbing him. As a matter of fact," Grice went on, with a glint in his eyes, "I thought that you might do something to wipe your nose clean."

"Oh," said Rollison, warily. "I comprehend. Aggressive policemen with ulterior motives, trying to scare me into unwilling co-operation. What?"

"You'd co-operate unwillingly with a man from Mars, nothing less," Grice said. "Find out what jewels McGinn has, will you? Try to get details, weights, measurements, settings. It's odd that McGinn doesn't show willing to let us look at them."

"And all will be forgiven?"

"All will be overlooked," Grice said severely.

"No action about Bella Daventry being at Wrightson's flat?"

"No, unless things alter a lot."

"We have struck a gentleman's agreement," declared the Toff, and promptly took Grice's right hand. Then he glanced at the telephone, as if willing it to ring. It rang. He shifted his position to lift the receiver and announced: "Richard Rollison here."

It was Mr. Millionaire McGinn.

"Why, if it isn't my great benefactor in person," boomed Connor McGinn, in a slightly less powerful voice than on the Saturday morning. "Mr. Rollison, sir, I hope you'll stay right there. I want to come and see you and express my thanks for your magnificent service on my behalf. Just stay—"

"May I come and see you instead?" asked Rollison humbly.

"Well, that's thoughtful of you," declared Connor McGinn. "That's very thoughtful indeed. Sure, I'll be waiting right here, and Rory will be with me. You can't get here soon enough, Mr. Rollison. You can't be a minute too soon."

"You're very good," said Rollison. "Goodbye for now." He rang off, and smiled at Grice, who must have heard that booming voice.

"When he knows you," Grice growled, "he'll want to take all that back."

"Still sour, Bill? And after I've taken such trouble for you. Jolly!"

Jolly came in at once.

"Did you see two photographs of an ugly man, and one of a set of prints in the dark room?" asked Rollison.

"Why, yes, sir. They are in separate envelopes on your desk."

Rollison investigated.

"So they are. Thanks. You may go. Bill," he said to Grice, "here's the chap who slugged Ebbutt, whose arm I broke, and—"

Grice grabbed.

"That's the chauffeur!" he exclaimed. "I had a picture of him from the office. He's new—name of Norris."

"That so?" asked Rollison, innocently. "Well, get him, Bill."

Grice started to ask a question, changed his mind, and hurried out.

As he went, Rollison thought of Bella, so nearly killed; and of the murderous strength of Black Norris.

Would Norris strike at the girl next?

Was she in danger, as Rollison believed? Or was Grice right?

Chapter Sixteen

The McGinns Together

"Well, well, well, *well!*" breathed Connor McGinn gustily, "so we meet at last, Mr. Rollison, we meet at last. This is a great day for me."

His great hand closed over Rollison's. It was unexpectedly firm. Standing, he was massive, and his paunch did not look anything like as well developed as it had on the bed the previous night.

In his way, he was a handsome man.

His hair was silvering, but his skin was as clear as the skin of a small boy, and ruddy, too. There was hardly a wrinkle on his face. He even used a little make-up, which startled Rollison; it was only a hint, but was unmistakable. He used a clean-smelling pomade, too. Six-foot two if he stood an inch, he was massive in a well-preserved way. His blue-grey suit, of Palm Beach cloth, fitted him perfectly. His cream-coloured collar, his tie with the diamond-studded pin, and everything about him exuded money.

His smile exuded goodwill.

When they had finished shaking hands, he took Rollison by the elbow and led him across the big room at the Miramar. There were hotels in the luxury class in many parts of London, but nothing remotely like this in its super luxury. Everything glittered and glistened, all carpets were like sponge rubber, all mirrors were gilded, all drinks cost as much as if they were poured out of bottles of Waterford glass into goblets stemmed with solid gold.

It was in Park Lane, overlooking Hyde Park, and the most expensive suites – which cost in a month the year's salary of an average man – had balconies on which one could sit, on warm days, and patronise the *hoi polloi* wandering in plebeian coat-sleeves or sitting on little green chairs and watching the traffic go by.

Judging by its opulent appearance, this was the royal suite.

Rory McGinn was by the open window leading to the balcony. He turned to smile. His chin was red and puffy in two places, and one eye was slightly bloodshot; that made the smile rather one-sided, but there was nothing except amiability in his eyes.

"Rory," declared McGinn, as if he wanted passing pedestrians to hear him, "here is Mr. Rollison, our very good friend Rollison. If it weren't for Mr. Rollison you know what would have happened to me?"

Rory said: "I can guess." He shook hands. "And I've forgiven him, too."

"Forgiven him, eh?" After a moment's startled pause McGinn slapped his thigh in delight. "Gee, I understand you now, Rory, he gave you that wallop on the chin. And you've forgiven him! Let me tell you, that's mighty handsome of you. Mr. Rollison," boomed McGinn, gripping Rollison's elbow tightly, "I'm going to tell you something, I'm going to tell you that my nephew has forgiven you. Ain't that grand?"

"Fine," said Rollison solemnly, "and dandy."

"What did I tell you, boy?" demanded McGinn of his handsome nephew, "Mr. Rollison has a fine sense of humour. Who was it said that the English hadn't any sense of humour? I know all about it, Mr. Rollison. Rory wanted to come with you, you weren't sure he could make the grade, so you walloped him. Rory's like me, he likes a man who knows what he wants and sets out to get it, don't you, boy?"

Rory grinned, a little awkwardly because his chin was so stiff.

"Now, what will you have to drink?" asked McGinn, with anxious hospitality. "Just give it a name."

"No, not now, thanks," said Rollison, "I've only just had breakfast."

He wondered what McGinn really wanted to say; whether the older man would wait until his nephew had gone before coming to the point. He was in no hurry. There were plenty of things to think about, and the main problem now was the problem of the jewels which McGinn claimed to have in his possession. That, and the fact that Arthur Rowe was missing, and that somewhere in London was brutish Black Norris, with a broken arm and, undoubtedly, a simmering hatred.

"Well, just say the word when you want a drink," insisted Connor McGinn. "Now, sir, I guess you know something of the problem on my mind. Rory's told you what he guessed, and he's a good guesser. Yes, sir. I had reason to believe that I was being played for a sucker, Mr. Rollison, by this firm of Fingleton. I met them when I was in England for a few days a month ago. Some of the jewels offered to me seemed like stolen gems. Yes, sir. You don't need telling that a man who collects precious stones has to keep a weather eye open, and I like to know what jewels have been stolen! I'm talking of big pieces, you understand. So I was cautious with this Paul Wrightson, and the whole firm of Fingleton. You blame me?"

"Certainly not."

"I didn't think you would," said McGinn, with satisfaction. He pulled up a large armchair and sat down slowly, smoothed his silvery hair, and smiled. His teeth were very good for a man who must be in the middle fifties at least.

Rory stood by his side, a young Adonis.

"Then my nephew liked the look of another director in this business—I haven't had the pleasure of meeting her yet, but I've seen her photograph. I don't believe she would knowingly mix with rogues, but I have to be *sure*. Eh, Rory?"

Rory nodded.

"So that's what I wanted you to do for me, Mr. Rollison, check on Fingletons. I told you that I'd heard that you were the best private eye—you don't object to being called a private eye?" McGinn became suddenly anxious.

"Not at all," murmured Rollison.

"That's fine! The best private eye in all of Europe," went on McGinn, relaxing, "and when I want anything, I want the best. Because I can pay for the best, Mr. Rollison. I was prepared to pay two hundred and fifty pounds as retainer for your service, but since then, things have changed. Yes, sir, they've changed. They've taken on a very different complexion, and I want to amend my offer. There are some things you can't measure in money, although money can show the depth of appreciation that is meant, Mr. Rollison. And let me make myself quite clear. First, you saved the life of my nephew, and that means more than most things to me. Then you rescued me. Now one of these scoundrels is still at large, and while I'm in England I want to feel absolutely safe. You see what I mean? I want protection and I want you to protect me, and I'm offering a retainer of one thousand pounds, plus all expenses and a proper fee for your time. And I hope you'll accept, Mr. Rollison."

Rory's smile suggested that he was quite sure that Rollison would accept.

Rollison was a long way from sure that he liked and trusted Rory McGinn. He had seen very little of the man, and that little in odd circumstances. Perhaps it was the smile; and perhaps there was nothing odd in Rory McGinn feeling a little supercilious at the thought that an Englishman of aristocratic lineage would jump at a new kind of dollar aid. Perhaps it was the coincidence of his arrival at the flat, the reluctance of a man to kill him and the convenient escape of Black Norris. It might have a little to do with the fact that he ran McGinn's London office, and so had employed Black Norris.

But he had taken risks for Bella; after laughing her warning away. It was Rory's smile which quickened Rollison's doubts, but—

"Well, what do you say?" McGinn asked.

Rollison said mildly: "I don't make terms, Mr. McGinn, you must talk about them with my man Jolly." He beamed. "And I don't take jobs unless I'm sure that there's plenty to do. Are you seriously afraid of being swindled?"

"Yes, sir," boomed McGinn, as if stung to vehemence. "This isn't the first time folk have tried to play me for a sucker, and I guess it won't be the last. I've been going into this Fingleton firm, and now

I understand that one of the directors, Wrightson himself, was undoubtedly a crook. If he tried to fix me one way, who's to say that others won't try also? I'm here to buy jewels in big quantities, Mr. Rollison, I'm right in the market. I want to make sure that I'm not swindled, and I want to make sure that I'm not robbed. Let me tell you, I need protection. Don't you agree, Rory?"

"Sure," Rory said, sliding a hand into his pocket. He wasn't smiling now, but watching Rollison closely.

"All right," Rollison said. "I'll play. But it'll cost you a hundred pounds extra, whatever terms Jolly fixes, for every day I have to miss the Oval."

McGinn chuckled. "Oh, the Test Match. It's going well, I guess. I understand, I'm just the same way over a ball game back home. Well, sir, you've relieved my mind a great deal, and now just to show you that I'm in earnest, I want to let you see some of my jewels—those which I bought on the Continent."

He got up, very light on his feet, very bright-eyed.

"Uncle!" Rory's voice was sharp.

"What's that, boy?"

"With the greatest respect," said Rory, looking at Rollison, "I don't think you should let Mr. Rollison see where you keep the jewels."

That was all.

Rory McGinn and Rollison eyed each other levelly, and the older McGinn looked mildly embarrassed. He moistened his lips, then pursed them, blew out a funny little popping breath, and turned away. He stalked out of the room.

Rollison began to smile. He didn't blame Rory; in fact, Rory was right, but what had made the man say that? Was he sore about the punch the previous night? Did he sense Rollison's doubts?

"Don't take me the wrong way," Rory said. "When Uncle Connor likes a guy, he trusts him completely."

"Uncle Connor's nephew Rory is a much wiser man," murmured Rollison, and turned to see Connor McGinn come in, carrying a large suitcase.

He could hardly believe it.

The suitcase had the oldest ancestor of hiding-places, a simple false bottom. Any professional thief would know exactly how to check inside and outside measurements, and, once a discrepancy was found, would have the hiding-place open in a few minutes. But Rollison kept a straight face. Rory McGinn shrugged. Without having said a word to him, Connor McGinn put the case on an armchair, and, with great deliberation, unlocked it, then touched springs which revealed the secret compartment.

Rollison could not fail to see all this.

McGinn lifted out a tray spread with wash-leather.

On the tray were jewels of glittering beauty; jewels which made Rollison catch his breath, because the blaze of light coming from them was so dazzling. Most of these stones were diamonds, but the blood-red richness of rubies and the blue purity of sapphires glowed among them.

"Aren't they lovely?" asked Connor McGinn, in a different, almost a cooing voice. He paused. "Sure, they're beautiful, just beautiful." He picked up a small diamond, held it between his fingers, smiled upon it, and then selected a sapphire. The smile on his full lips was the smile of a lover upon the beloved. "Just beautiful," he repeated, softly.

The door opened.

"That's more than I can say for any of you," a man said, and stepped in. Behind him was a girl dressed in the uniform of a maid at the Miramar. "Get away from those jewels, McGinn. Keep back, Rollison. Okay, Liz, go get 'em."

Chapter Seventeen

McGinn And Another Debt

Man and girl were masked, not with scarves, but with stiff brown paper, cut so that there were large holes for the eyes, and fitting over the nose, stopping just at the upper lip. They looked young. The girl had a figure which most, men would dream about, and when she moved she showed the hip movement of Marilyn Monroe. She was that kind of size, too; small but nicely rounded. The man had a cloth cap on; he looked and sounded young and very confident, and his gun didn't show any sign of quivering.

McGinn backed slowly, stiffly, away from the diamonds.

"No," he said, in a choky kind of voice. "No, please don't—"

"Pick 'em up, Liz," the masked man said.

The girl was close to the table and the suitcase, now, and she took a large wash-leather bag from the capacious pocket of her lavender-blue uniform. She started to pick up the jewels.

"Don't do that!" cried McGinn.

He moved forward, swiftly, lightly. Two things happened at once, with a third a split second late. The man squeezed the trigger, a bullet snapped out but made little noise; this was an airgun. McGinn stopped in his tracks, and Rory McGinn cried: "Uncle, get back, get back!" and sounded terrified.

He hadn't moved.

The girl jumped away from the tray.

"Next time you'll get a bullet where it hurts," the masked young man said to Connor McGinn. "I don't want to harm you, but those diamonds are changing owners. You can afford it."

No one spoke.

The eyes behind the mask turned towards Rollison.

"Very quiet, aren't you?" he asked, mockingly. "I thought that the great Toff always had the answer to surprises like this. Don't you keep a blow-pipe and poisoned dart in the hollow of your cheek? Or shoot fire with your eyes? Or wear a chain waistcoat which makes you indifferent to mere bullets and slugs?"

Rollison said mildly: "You know too much, pal."

In spite of the situation, the man with the gun laughed. The McGinns didn't. They were now remarkably alike in pallor and attitude. Connor McGinn was breathing noisily through parted lips, and staring at the girl's nimble fingers as she packed the jewels in the bag. Rory McGinn was gaping at the gun, as if he were concerned only with the danger.

"You don't know enough," the young man said. "Get a move on, Liz. Okay? Now, the three of you, turn round and face the window. Don't—"

Rollison leapt for the window.

It was only three feet away from him, and wide open. He reached it as he heard the hissing sound of a bullet coming his way, but he felt no pain. Once on the balcony, he slammed the doors behind him. Net curtains behind the glass hid the people in the room. He couldn't fasten the doors, couldn't shut the young thief in, but the thief had to cope with the McGinns. He couldn't write off Connor McGinn as he might his nephew.

Rollison roared: "Thief! Stop thief! Police!"

He was only fifty feet above the street, and on the instant twenty or thirty people turned and stared up.

"Room Fifty-one!" he roared. "Tell police, *Room Fifty-one.*" He was moving towards the next balcony, which was about six feet away.

He climbed up on to the wall of this, and jumped.

He heard people screaming down below. Brakes squealed as motorists were held up by crowds surging into the road. A police whistle shrilled.

Rollison sailed through the air, knowing that he would fall fifty feet to cold, deadly stone if he missed his footing.

He landed on a six-inch edge, and swayed backwards; below, there was more terrified screaming. He hovered there, with disaster waiting with open arms. Gradually, he swayed forward. Then it was over, and he was safe.

He heard another scream as he jumped down on to the next balcony. He pulled open the double doors, and ran into a room as luxuriously appointed as Connor McGinn's. A telephone stood on a table, and he was speaking into it within ten seconds, only slightly out of breath.

"There are thieves in Room Fifty-one," he said. "Please have the passages barricaded off, lifts and staircases watched. The thieves are armed."

"*Armed*, sir." A girl operator gasped.

"Did you understand?"

"Oh, yes, at once—"

"That's fine," said Rollison. He banged the receiver down and went towards the next room, which led to the passage. The door was closed, but he could hear sounds, as of men running; or of scuffling. He took a gun out of his coat pocket, opening the door carefully, and stared out.

His tension fell away.

One big plain-clothes man from Scotland Yard was holding the masked Liz, by the shoulders, and she was struggling furiously and hacking at his shins with her high heels. The man kept shifting from one foot to the other, showing remarkable self-control; but suddenly he bent her double and slapped her bottom resoundingly. She went still.

Grice had his left wrist handcuffed to the masked man's, and held the bag of jewels in his right. Two other Yard men were disappearing into McGinn's room. Connor McGinn was coming out. At first dazed and bewildered, he suddenly became wildly joyful, and snatched at the jewels. A startled Grice let them go.

Rory wasn't in sight.

"Hallo, Bill," said Rollison, brightly, "I couldn't be more pleased if you were going to give me the freedom of the Yard. I knew you were quick, but not so quick. Realise what was cooking?"

Grice said: "We don't sleep all the time."

"Now, we're friends, remember?"

"I remember," Grice said. He flicked a glance at McGinn, who was dipping his hands into the jewel bag as if to make sure that the precious treasures were there. "We knew this woman took a job here yesterday, and we'd heard of her before, so we kept an eye on her." He leaned forward to the girl named Liz, and pulled the brown-paper mask off. She wasn't a chicken at all, nearer forty than thirty; and Rollison marvelled at her figure. "She'll never learn to keep her fingers clean," Grice went on, "but she did three years not long ago—for a job with a man named Norris."

He looked swiftly at McGinn, who showed not the slightest comprehension. Rollison smiled faintly.

Liz suddenly hacked at her captor's shin, then spat at Grice; she didn't miss.

"… shrew," Grice said, with commendable self-restraint, and took out a handkerchief.

Suddenly, Connor McGinn looked up. He clutched the neck of the bag as a dipsomaniac would clutch the neck of the last bottle of whisky in existence. He did not appear to see anyone except Grice. In a strangely quiet and dignified voice, he said: "Superintendent Grice, I shall always be in your debt. These jewels are irreplaceable. Thank you, sir, thank you indeed."

He turned and went back into his apartment, and Rollison glanced in. Rory McGinn was by the window, with his face to it; so Rollison couldn't see his expression, although he guessed what it was like.

Rory said: "Uncle, I guess I'm all kinds of a heel, but I just couldn't take it. That gun—"

"Don't worry, boy," said Connor McGinn, still with his strange, uncharacteristic mildness. "No great harm has been done, and you must not flagellate yourself over your own shortcomings." In that moment he was almost as precise as Jolly. He paused, jewels in hand, then turned slowly and espied Rollison. He smiled. "Do come in, Mr. Rollison," he invited. "I just have to tell you how much I appreciate your swift action. I understand your reputation much more than I did, sir. Such courage—"

"Oh, hell!" exclaimed Rory McGinn. He swung away from the window, strode out, pushed past Grice, who made no attempt to stop him, and went careering down the passage.

Connor McGinn looked positively sad.

"Poor Rory," he said. "Shall I let you into a family secret, Mr. Rollison?" He put the bag of jewels down on the suitcase, and went on in his subdued voice: "Rory watched his own mother drown. He just could not find the courage to dive into one of the Adirondack lakes to save her. It will always be a cross for him. Since then he has flagellated himself because of his lack of physical courage. I still hope that one day he will conquer it. Last night, of course, you were quite right in the way you treated him, although you can readily understand how bitter it was for him."

"Yes, I can see," Rollison conceded. "He has his good moments, though."

Connor McGinn became more his booming self. "What do you mean, sir? What kind of moments?"

"Earlier last night," said Rollison, and told McGinn what had happened at the bungalow.

McGinn whistled softly to himself as he listened, and seemed deeply pleased. He was posing most of the time, of course; he was a born poseur, and loved to dramatise himself and events.

"What do you think of Bella Daventry?" he asked softly.

"They don't come any lovelier."

"Really? Well, well, that's very interesting," said McGinn. "When one comes to think, it is possible to imagine that seeing the girl in danger, Rory was immediately reminded of his mother and for once he conquered the physical timidity which has been the curse of his life. I would very much like to see this young lady. I wonder if she is as honest as she is prepossessing."

"Meet her, and judge for yourself," Rollison suggested dryly. He moved across the room and picked up the jewels. "You've got to find something better than a false bottom in a suitcase," he prognosticated, "let's see if we can get any idea."

There was a tap at the door, and Grice came in. He made a beeline for the jewels, and asked if he could check that they were all present. McGinn said, humbly, that he could do whatever he liked, that if the police thought it wise, he could deposit them in a safe deposit, or the hotel safe. He seemed shaken by this clear evidence of his own carelessness. He was a big, plump, handsome, outwardly worried man, but gradually his self-confidence returned, his voice grew louder until it was positively booming.

Before Rollison left he had agreed to dine with the McGinns and to bring Bella Daventry.

Rollison did not go straight back to Gresham Terrace, but drove first to the East End. A Sabbath calm reigned at the gymnasium, due to Mrs. Ebbutt's convictions. She had left her spouse for the Citadel, too, but two cronies, including Charlie, shared his liquid solace.

A conical lump, nicely wrapped in sticking-plaster, decorated the back of his head.

He had a lot to say about his assailant, too; but he was cheerfully contemplating tomorrow's cricket.

On the way home, Rollison called at Scotland Yard. Here, men in plain clothes and men in uniform greeted him as they would an old friend, and he beamed upon them all. He was permitted to go to Grice's long, narrow room, overlooking the Embankment. When he entered, it was sunlight. A beam of sun shone on Grice's plastered hair, making him look quite distinguished.

"The sun and the righteous," Rollison burbled. "I didn't know about you before. McGinn's jewels all honestly come by?"

"Not a shadow of doubt," said Grice. He tapped a manilla folder on his desk. "I've had them checked against invoices which were approved by Customs. Everything's genuine. You know, Roily"—he sat back and he was now in a most amiable mood, which served to show the stimulating effect of a little success—"the Fingleton crowd is the one to watch, including the girl."

"No doubt at all," murmured Rollison. "Every man should watch Bella Daventry and learn the truth of beauty."

"One of these days you're going to allow a girl with a pretty face and a ripe figure to ruin your reputation. Where'd you get those fingerprints and Norris's photograph?"

"He came to see me. I won."

"And you let him go? What a lunatic you can be!"

"As a matter of fact, he was helped—while I was busy at Heybridge. I'd hoped to bring him to you on a plate—"

"Next time, just bring him."

"Readily," promised Rollison, with fervour. "What's his record like?"

"Ugly. He was first put inside in Durban, twelve years or so ago. He came back here – he's a Londoner – and did three years for robbery with violence. Liz was his stooge, then. The man we caught at the Miramar was in the same mob."

"And Arthur Rowe?"

"I can't get anything on him," Grice said, worriedly. "Either Bella Daventry can't draw word pictures, or she won't give him away. Watch that girl, she'd be in custody if it weren't for you."

"Guilty, sir."

"There's just one possibility about Rowe," said Grice, abruptly. "Norris was working with a man named Jenkinson in South Africa. Norris got four years, Jenkinson seven. I've cabled South Africa for a photograph of Jenkinson. He might be this mysterious Rowe."

"Worth trying," Rollison agreed.

"Thanks," Grice said, sarcastically. "Now listen to me for a change. *Don't* let Bella Daventry fool you. She knows where Rowe is."

Very slowly, Rollison stood up.

"No, Superintendent," he said meekly. "I won't be fooled. Good day to you."

He walked thoughtfully through the Yard and out to his Rolls-Bentley. It was a lovely day, although there were big white clouds and quite a wind. It was hot when the sun came out, pleasantly cool when it went in. He looked up at great patches of blue sky, and they reminded him of sapphires and of the eyes of Bella Daventry.

What did Grice know?

Could he be sure that Bella was bad?

Was she?

If not, why was she so determined to shield Rowe?

He pondered all of these things as he lunched in the Sabbath hush of his Club. His one conclusion was that he would prefer to trust Bella than Rory McGinn.

Was she in danger?

Rowe had tried to kill her, although she had denied it. If Rowe wanted her dead—

Suddenly, Rollison was in a hurry to get back to his flat.

Chapter Eighteen

Dinner For Four

When Rollison reached Gresham Terrace it was a little after four o'clock. Jolly had seen him coming, and opened the door. He looked pleased with himself; and it was not the first time that a pretty girl had had that effect on Jolly.

So all was well.

Bella was in the big room, sitting on the desk, swinging one slim, enticing leg. She looked round at Rollison. Her eyes had the sky in them. She smiled, and her lips told of radiance and seemed to tell of loveliness of spirit, too. She stood up. He went to her, holding out both hands, and she took them. He looked at her very steadily, searching those eyes for the slightest hint of deception, and he saw none.

"How sober you are," she said.

"Thoughts," declared Rollison. "It's only now and again that I get a chance of kissing the loveliest girl in the world." He kissed her lightly on each cheek; and his heart began to pound. "Better?"

"Much! I've been"—she turned to the trophy wall, and looked from the top-hat to the hempen rope and to many other exhibits at the same time—"I've been hearing about your exploits."

"Jolly's fired," announced the Toff.

She laughed. "I think he worships you."

"I fancy you exaggerate," said the Toff, and chuckled. "But I know what you mean. You remember Rory McGinn vaguely, I suppose."

"Oh, yes." That sobered her.

"Remember his uncle?"

She moved a little farther away from him, and frowned. They were quiet for a few seconds, and Rollison waited for her to break the silence, trying to judge exactly what she was thinking; and he knew that was impossible, it was just that her beauty made him reject any idea that she could be bad.

"I've never met Connor McGinn," she declared. "Mr. Rollison, don't you believe me?"

He grinned, suddenly, and his whole face lit up.

"Whether I do or whether I don't, I'll have the law on you if you call me Mister again! Richard it may be; if you really have a heart, you can make it Rolly. Not that I can expect too much—that face, that figure and a heart as well."

After another pause, Bella said: "I think I can understand why some people could dislike you."

"As on the famous afternoon at the Oval! Bella, listen." He took her hands in a swift movement, imprisoning them. "Do you know where Arthur Rowe is?"

"No!"

"I hope that's true. I don't know that I would blame you if you lied for him, but I would blame you if you lied so that it would hurt him. I think he's in a bad spot. If he's innocent of all this, it's a very bad one. If I met him, I might be able to help."

"You'd give him up to the police."

"No," said Rollison. "No, I wouldn't, Bella. Not the first time."

She swallowed hard. "How—how can I be sure?"

"Take me on trust. Remember that it might be that Arthur Rowe is being framed. I don't say he is, I do say he could be. And if he is, you are, too. Grice thinks you're shielding him."

"I don't know where Arthur is," Bella said. "That's the simple truth."

There was a moment of silence, before Rollison squeezed her hands and let them go.

"All right, my sweet, that's the truth and all about it. It won't be the first time Grice has been wrong. Now, news! You're going to extend your list of acquaintances tonight. You're going to meet Uncle Connor. Think you can stand it?"

She flushed. "Does Rory know?"

"He does."

"Then I'll go," Bella said.

"Of course you'll go, that isn't the problem. What are you going to wear?"

"Wear?"

"They'll dress, and we can't have them disappointed in our Bella, can we? Black," he added, almost dreamily, "black, off those wonderful shoulders, flared, with a pale blue orchid to match your eyes. You could go to Rye Street."

"You're being silly. I haven't a black dress, anyhow, and I don't see the need to dress up."

"At the Miramar? Think, my Bella!" He eyed her up and down. With any other man, she would have felt herself blushing, but there was nothing impudent or insolent about his look, he was almost impersonal. He nodded. "I think Jolly has just the job," he said. "Come and see."

She didn't argue, but followed him.

Hanging in the wardrobe of her little room was a black evening-gown of shiny silk beneath beautiful lace. Obviously she fell in love with it the moment she saw it. She knew, too, that it must have cost a fortune. There were evening-shoes, a small bag and everything she needed. She was touched with a kind of false excitement while she looked these things over, during tea, and then while she dressed.

The dress fitted her.

Jolly, by some magic, had produced a huge corsage of sapphire blue from a flower shop which should have been shut. And Jolly was discursive. The dress belonged to a niece of Mr. Rollison's who lived in the country. It was to be a present. She would never know that it had been worn.

It all sounded almost convincing.

Bella went into the big room when she was ready.

Rollison, wearing a white tuxedo, was sitting at the desk, writing. At the first rustle of sound he looked up. His hand stopped moving. He didn't get up, just stared; and all she wanted to see was in his eyes; deep, profound admiration for a lovely woman.

It was a strange moment, and she wanted it to linger. Words would spoil it, but she wondered what he would say.

He rose, slowly, put the pen down with great deliberation and, without a smile, except in his eyes, rounded the table and came towards her. Then she knew what he was going to do; and knew that it was right. He reached her, took her slowly, so very slowly in his arms, and kissed her. She felt as if all she had ever known about men's embraces were like a child's knowledge of life. In an odd, convincing way, she knew that it wasn't because Rollison wanted to kiss and hold a woman, it went much deeper than that. She knew that she mattered. She also knew that it was absurd, and sensed that their lives would touch swiftly and briefly, and then part company.

He let her go.

"I think," he said, "that I hope you don't love him."

She did not need telling that he meant Rory McGinn.

Two plain-clothes men from the Yard were in the entrance hall of the Miramar. One was at the lift on the second floor landing. One was outside Suite 51. A footman, made available by the hotel for occasions, opened the door. Rory McGinn came forward to meet Rollison and Bella, tall and strikingly handsome in a way which matched the Toff. He seemed to have put his inhibitions behind him, his smile was quite free, and there was no hint of antagonism as he looked at Rollison.

"I think you two have met," said Rollison dryly.

"You can take it from me that I don't have to be reminded," Rory said, and took Bella's hand. His eyes sent the same message as Rollison's; she knew that she looked superb. Here were two men, each without a peer, immaculate and courteous and intent on pleasing her.

Shadows lightened.

She did not know how close was the shadow of the Yard.

They went into the big room overlooking the park. It was still daylight, and one window was open. A cocktail cabinet was in one corner, and the footman went to it. They ordered drinks. The footman left them. In an unexpected way, none of them had much to say.

"My uncle won't be long," Rory said, after a while. "I can't think what's keeping him."

He waited for five minutes, then got up, said he would see if he could help his uncle, and left Bella and the Toff alone.

Rollison was smiling, at the way Bella's gaze followed Rory. In a foolish way, it hurt. He wished he knew the truth about her. Was she good, was she bad? Was she working with Rowe, did she know that he was a rogue?

She turned to look at him, and drove suspicion away.

Then Rory came striding back.

"Rollison, he's sick," he cried. "We've got to send for a doctor. He looks terrible."

Chapter Nineteen

Sick Man

"No doubt about it at all," said the hotel doctor, "he's suffering from some kind of irritant poisoning. Be all right now, mind you." McGinn had had an emetic which had acted violently; and some medicine. He contemplated the patient, who was breathing heavily, looking very pale and washed out, but quite alert; then he contemplated Rollison. "I shall analyse the stomach content, of course. Meanwhile, he must rest. I'll have a mixture made up. Hydrated oxide of iron, magnesia and—hum—castor oil. A little liquid tonight, that's all. Just a little liquid." He looked worriedly at McGinn, and announced: "I can't understand it. Ahem. I must be getting along."

He went ...

"Rollison," said McGinn, in a weak voice, "don't spoil that young woman's evening, go and see she has a good time."

"She's doing fine with Rory. She'll do much better with him than with me," Rollison assured him. "I didn't intend to stay long, anyhow, I've several things to do." He had now. "How are you feeling?"

"Weak as a kitten, but they haven't finished me yet. No, sir." McGinn's eyes looked huge in his flabby face. He turned his head slightly, and his voice became husky. "What can they want to kill me for? Who'd want to kill me by poisoning, can you answer me that?"

"I can find out," said Rollison. "Now take it easy. Like a police nurse?"

"Perhaps it would be a good idea," McGinn conceded. "Rollison, you're a wonderful help, I won't ever forget it. If you were my own flesh and blood—"

"Cut out lush sentiment," Rollison said briskly, and grinned and turned away. "I'll be seeing you."

He went across the hall and into the big room, where a table was laid for four. Candles were on it, as yet unlit. Darkness had fallen, except for the afterglow, and there was subdued side lighting in the room. It brought out the beauty of the girl and the good looks of Rory McGinn.

Rory jumped up from the settee.

"How is he?"

"He'll be all right," Rollison said, "and he still wants you to look after Bella." He beamed at her. "I don't blame him! I hope you'll forgive me, I've several things to do."

"You'll have dinner with us," Rory said quickly.

"Do you mind if I don't?" asked Rollison. "There's more to do than I expected, and I don't want to charge your uncle up for a day not at the Oval! Explain that to Bella." He raised his hand in salutation to Bella, smiled at Rory, and went out.

In his pocket were two bottles; one of aspirins, one of dyspepsia tablets, both taken from the bedside table in Connor McGinn's room.

Rowe – if the man was Rowe – could strike swiftly and savagely. Thrice in a day he had beaten a police watch; if he really wanted to kill Bella, could she be saved?

"For once you've been sensible," Grice said, taking the bottles, "don't say I haven't acknowledged it."

They were at the Yard.

Rollison had gone to Grice's Chelsea flat, and they had left there together. The tablets were to be analysed in the Yard laboratory, and the hotel doctor had been asked to send his report and the stomach contents to the Yard, for further analysis and corroboration.

Rollison had had a snack in the Yard canteen, thinking of the splendour of the dinner at the Miramar.

Now, he looked down at Grice's desk.

"All right," he said, "you've acknowledged my reformation. Your magnanimity has to be felt to be believed." He drew at a cigarette. "Did you expect an attack on McGinn?"

Grice said: "No, I can't say I did. After he was shanghaied and drugged, I thought they wanted him alive. But if you're really asking me whether I know what this is about, no. I'm as mystified as you are. I've got the Home Office prodding me every few hours because McGinn's such a big shot on the other side, and after this—" He broke off. "If I don't get results quickly—"

"You'll have to miss the Oval!"

"Don't be a flippant ass!"

"Oh, my Bill," protested Rollison, earnestly, "I can't imagine greater punishment. I want to get it over soon, too. A hit for six, Bill Ebbutt asked for, but I can't see it coming tonight. Any trace of Arthur Rowe?"

"No."

"News from South Africa?"

"That'll probably take days."

"Dare I ask what you got out of that pair who worked the trick at the Miramar this morning?"

"They both said the same thing. Rowe sent them. Rowe told them you'd be there. It was all done by telephone. They were to put the fear of death into you and the others, and look for the jewels if it didn't mean taking too many risks. They say that the only time they've met Rowe has been at the bungalow, and they haven't seen him in person for months. They used to work with him, and lately they've been on their own. Norris dug them out for this job. One thing sticks out a mile."

Grice looked sour when he said all this.

"Which thing?"

"Rowe wouldn't put up a show like this for a trifle. He thinks there's really big money."

"Sure it's Rowe?"

"*What?*" Grice came as near as he ever did to gasping. "Too much Rowe, for my liking," Rollison said. "Rowe in the murky background, Rowe with the right history, Rowe named by everyone and defended stoutly only by Bella Daventry. I don't know, but it seems a surfeit of Rowe. As if he's being put up as the Aunt Sally."

"All right. Name the chief crook."

"No can do," said Rollison sadly. "Oh, I grant that you have to look for Rowe, but—"

"Thanks," said Grice, heavily. "And we're looking! There is just one witness who might be able to tell us more, if she can be made to talk. She talked to you?" Grice was brusque.

"No more about Rowe. She can't tell us where he is."

"That's what you think," Grice said. "I'm going to pull her in soon. If she won't come for questioning without raising an argument, I'll find a charge. And you can't do anything to stop it."

Rollison went very still.

"Have you sent for her?"

"My men should be at the Miramar now."

"Oh," said Rollison, thinly. "Poor Bella. Poor Grice, Bamboozled by the pundits into making more misery for a girl who can't help herself. It's a great pity." There was no friendliness, no emotion at all in his voice. "This is where we part company in this job. According to my lights, I've tried to be helpful. From this time on, I keep my secrets."

He stood up.

"You'll be a fool if you do," Grice said.

"I was a fool to tell you that I saw Bella Daventry at that flat. If I hadn't, you couldn't rig up a charge. Not like you, Bill. You'd better look in at the Oval, to see how the game's played." Rollison's smile was bleak, as he moved towards the door.

Grice said: "All right, be sour. But that girl was with Paul Wrightson when he died. We've only your word for the way it happened. His prints were on the handle, but we know she wore gloves. This wouldn't be the first time you've lied to save a girl. So she's coming in and she's going to talk. She knows where Rowe is. I'm going to find him."

"Not through Bella."

"She's made you think not." Grice didn't get up from the desk, but he opened a folder, and on it was an enlargement of the photographs which Rollison had taken of the big man the previous night; and a sheet of fingerprints. "Before you go breathing vengeance, have a look at this."

He held out the photograph.

Rollison took it, turned it over, and read the caption pasted on the back; it was really a dossier. It did not make good reading. He glanced at the unsmiling Grice, who nodded, as if to confirm that everything on that slip of paper pasted to the back of the photograph was true.

Black Norris, Born 1908, originally heavy-weight champion British Armed Forces, twice convicted of robbery with violence, once in Durban, Natal, South Africa. Exceptionally powerful, known to be vicious, vindictive and with homicidal tendencies. Frequently works with others. Officers knowingly dealing with this man should use extreme care and in all cases apply for permission to carry firearms.

Rollison didn't speak.

"And you beat him twice, breaking his arm the second time," Grice said flatly. "I think he'll come for you. He may not do the job himself, but he'll try to kill you. I don't know who he's working with these days, except that he was at Rowe's bungalow a few days ago."

"Sure?"

"Yes, and I don't deal in maybes," Grice said. "For your own good, I'm having you followed, and I'm having the flat watched too. I'm justified, because Black Norris might have a cut at you, and I want him as badly as I want Rowe. If you try any tricks, or slip my men, it's your own look-out. I may not be able to carry on my job exactly according to your book of regulations," Grice added, almost nastily, "but I don't want to see you dead. I certainly don't want to see you killed by a brute like Norris over a girl whose blue eyes have hypnotised you."

Rollison found himself smiling.

"If missing, look for me at the Members' Stand, Kennington Oval, London, S.E.11," he said. "I'll keep a weather eye open for your chaps, and try not to shock 'em too much."

Grice didn't speak.

Rollison went on in the same tone: "And Bill—look after Bella. I think she's on the spot. You've seen how these people move—swift and deadly. Look after her. If you let her go, give her a guard. Understand?"

Grice said: "I heard you, anyhow."

Rollison went out and along the wide, brightly lighted corridors, and men who passed him and smiled were startled to see the grimness of his expression. Occasionally he acknowledged someone; most of the time he stared straight ahead. He reached the main entrance hall of the Criminal Investigation Department Building, and went downstairs and outside there, although his car was by the Civil Police building. He stood by the car, moving only when another turned into the wide entrance; but only one man was at the wheel. Another arrived, and three men got out. A third pulled closer to him, and he saw Bella sitting next to a big man in plain clothes. He moved swiftly, so that when she was out, and standing by the side of the car, he was nearer than the police.

"Bella," he said, "I thought I could avoid it. If heaven and earth can be made to move, I'll move them to clear you."

She looked at him through eyes which might have been cut out of blue ice. Then she turned and put a hand on the arm of a plain-clothes man, who led the way towards the steps and into the building.

Rollison watched her go.

He turned towards his car, not noticing that another had pulled up just outside – had actually come towards the iron gates so that to get back on to the Embankment, it would have to reverse. A big sign, clear in the headlights, read: *Metropolitan Police, No Entry.* A big man came hurrying from this car, and at first Rollison felt the flame of fear, for Grice's warning about Black Norris was vivid in his mind.

But it was Rory McGinn.

"Rory—" he began.

Rory stopped short, turned, recognised him in the well-lighted Yard, and hesitated for a moment. Only for a moment. He looked venomous; so great was his rage that it distorted his features, robbed him of handsomeness.

"So that's the way you helped her," he growled, and flashed his right fist. Rollison was too late to dodge, but moved his head swiftly; the clenched fist caught him a glancing blow. Off his balance, he staggered. Rory hit him again, landing on his chest where the knuckle-duster had made its wound, and it hurt agonisingly.

Two constables came running.

"What's all this, please?"

"Stop that!"

Rory turned away.

Rollison stood watching him, as the pain gradually eased. Rory disappeared up the stone steps, and Rollison got into his car and drove out of the Yard, on to the Embankment, round Parliament Square and then across St. James's Park, deserted except for lovers, towards Gresham Terrace.

He felt sick at heart; and the sickness possessed him even while he was getting out of the car and walking towards the front door of the house.

Then sickness was swallowed up in one gulping moment of fear.

A big, dark-clad figure appeared from the doorway and blocked his path. He knew at once that it was Black Norris. He knew that he hadn't a chance. Flinging himself to one side was almost instinctive. He heard shouts, saw the vivid flash from a gun, fell heavily, and feared death.

Chapter Twenty

Self-Denial For The Toff

Feet scuffled, men shouted, a whistle blew, a shot roared. Rollison heard these things as he lay crouching on the ground, head covered by his arms, hope desperate in him, and the fear still deep.

A woman shouted and started to cry, men came running, car engines sounded like racing models, the whistle blew again, the scuffling of feet drew much nearer to the Toff. Dust rose from the steps, a man kicked him on the side of the head and made his ears ring, someone trod on his leg, unbalanced, and fell, cursing.

"Get away!" a different man cried in a clear, commanding voice. "Clear a way!"

That was Jolly.

Suddenly, Rollison knew that Jolly was bending over him, protectingly, probably feeling hopeless and helpless and fearful, but on the spot. The scuffling reached a furious crescendo, but soon something cracked and a thud came – and after that, all that could be heard was the heavy breathing of several men and the car engines, ticking over now, and a few people hurrying.

"Mr. Rollison," Jolly began, "Mr. Rollison—"

Something metallic clicked sharply.

"Well, that's got him," a man said, deep with satisfaction. "Well put him where he won't do any more harm. Have a look at the Toff."

"Mr. Rollison—"

"Dazed," said Rollison, weakly. "Bruised. Battered. Trodden on. Shaken. Scared out of my wits. I don't ever want to be nearer death, but I'm all right, Jolly."

He struggled to a kneeling position, looking into Jolly's face, and he saw that it was deathly pale, and that the doleful brown eyes were glistening, suspiciously wet. Now and again, some incident like this told Rollison how Jolly felt, and he remembered Bella's emphatic: "I think he worships you." Well, she didn't, any longer. And just as well, baby snatching was out.

Two Yard men ranged themselves by Rollison's side, hauled him up, and, each with a hand on his arm, helped him toward the door. Jolly came after them, slowly, like a man who had been through a great physical exertion. By the door, two men were standing over Black Norris, who was sitting with his back against the wall, handcuffed to a plain-clothes man who had to squat. Norris, one arm in plaster, looked dazed; but he caught sight of Rollison and glared with unbridled hatred.

A Yard man said: "Well, Rollison, that's one life you owe us!" He was almost chuckling with relief.

"Ah, yes, thanks," said Rollison. "Especially Grice. Beer all round—no, damn it, let's be big-hearted, we'll all have an evening together soon. Next week, say, to celebrate the victory."

"What victory?"

"Didn't you know? We're playing Australia."

A man laughed, and said: "You can't beat him, can you?" in a tone which suggested reluctant admiration.

Then another by Rollison's side, and still holding his arm, asked hopefully: "Can you manage now?"

"Oh, yes, thanks. Still self-propelled."

"Not hurt?"

"Just my pride."

"Never mind your pride, you were damned lucky," the man said. "He was waiting for you in the front room downstairs. Must have been there since last night. The tenants are away. He meant to kill you, and we've got him for attempted murder at least. Just for a minute, I thought we'd failed. Two of us were watching when he came out, and if I hadn't—"

They were at the foot of the stairs.

"Don't be so modest," chided Rollison, "if you hadn't what?"

"Seen his gun, and shouted," said the Yard man. "Spoiled his aim, I think."

"For ever grateful," said Rollison, and surprised himself by chuckling. He was a little bewildered and unsteady, from the succession of shocks. "Like Connor McGinn. Watch Connor McGinn, we daren't lose him."

He swayed.

He knew that someone helped him upstairs, that he was taken to his bedroom, that he was undressed; and only Jolly would do that. He felt foolish, weak and peculiarly frightened; as if he could never live down the fright that had come when Norris had walked out of his own house with that gun. Well, Norris had tried, failed, and was on his way to a cell; he wouldn't see freedom again for many years, if ever he saw it at all. But would he talk? Would he involve Rowe and others?

Rollison didn't think so.

That was the beginning of the return of reason.

He could even be glad that Bella was in custody; and safe.

A pale and subdued Jolly brought him hot, sweet coffee. Grice telephoned inquiries through a sergeant. Three newspapers telephoned and four reporters called; Jolly dealt with all these. He also gave Rollison two tablets, and Rollison took them obediently and, soon afterwards, went to sleep.

It was a lovely Monday morning.

A strange thing happened in London. Much, much earlier than was their wont, some thirty-five thousands souls rose from snug beds, looked out the windows, saw a blue sky with hints of grey cirrus, the kind of sky that promised fine weather. So, rejoicing, they prepared their own breakfasts and, in most cases, left their wives, their mothers, their sisters and small brothers, and began the trek towards Kennington. They went by Tube, train, bus, Green

Line, car, coach, bicycle and tricycle, motor-bike, motor-scooter and Shanks's pony. Two went on stilts.

By six o'clock, many thousands were already outside the grounds, four deep, hugging the dark, inhospitable walls of the Oval, looking up at the swollen gasometers in their fresh green paint, seeing the flags of Australia and the United Kingdom flying side by side. People in the nearby houses overlooking the ground still slept, but the crowd, swollen by hundreds every few seconds, began its long wait, opened paper-bags, ate, smoked, read, bought newspapers, magazincs, fruit gums and peppermints, drank tea and coffee out of Thermos flasks, Pepsi-cola, lemonade, ginger beer and even cold tea.

Among these, in a small, compact group, were twelve men from Ebbutt's gymnasium, and at their head was Ebbutt, his lump a little deflated, his round face ruddy, his patience inexhaustible and, although he admitted it to no man, his 'conscience a little uneasy. He was planning to telephone Rollison directly he got into the ground.

Minute by minute, the crowd massed.

At half-past nine the gates were opened, and the vast crocodile, winding round dozens of streets and hundreds of houses, carrying folding stools, seats, coats, mackintoshes, bags, food for a day and hopeful hearts, began to move.

At that hour, Rollison woke.

The first thing Rollison realised was that his head was much clearer than he had any right to expect, which was undoubtedly due to Jolly's tablets. Then, that it was a fine day, and play—

He remembered Norris, and all that had gone before. That sobered him. He remembered the Test Match score-cards, and wondered why Black Norris and little Lemaitre had spent part of Saturday at the Oval. He did a great deal of thinking, and was interrupted when Jolly came in, creeping and stealthy; seeing Rollison's alert eyes, he rose erect.

"Good morning, sir."

"Hallo, Jolly. Thanks."

"Don't mention it, sir." The brown eyes, their shadowy fear gone, looked hard at Rollison. "You appear to be *much* better. I'll bring in the tea and the newspapers." He went out, and Rollison smiled and lit his first cigarette. Three minutes later, the tea-tray was by his side, the newspapers open on the bed, and the post – five letters in all – was by his right hand.

He opened the letters while snatching glances at the headlines. None surprised him. There was the story of the attempt to take McGinn's jewels, the sensational escapade at the Miramar and, fantastically, a picture said to be of him jumping from balcony to balcony, taken by some enthusiastic amateur who had pointed, pressed and hoped, and so made himself some pin money.

There was the story of McGinn's poisoning, and of the attack on Rollison, and the arrest of Black Norris.

"It is understood", the newspapers said, "that the Toff was not seriously hurt. Mr. Connor McGinn had recovered from the worst of the ill effects of the suspected poisoning by midnight. He told the P.A. that he was anxious to finish his business in England and return to the United States, 'where I can get some peace and quiet that I don't seem to get around here'."

Rollison read more closely, and when Jolly came in, looked up and said: "Nothing about Miss Daventry?"

"No, sir."

"Found anything out?"

"No, sir. Mr. Ebbutt telephoned, a few minutes ago, to say that he will be by the gasometer-side score-board all day; he appears to have obtained a good viewpoint. His friends are with him, and if they are required he will willingly come to see you."

Rollison grinned. "Willingly?"

"No doubt he will come, sir."

"We must try to leave him in peace and quiet," said the Toff. "Is Grice—?"

The front-door bell rang. Jolly bowed himself out, and Rollison glanced at the letters, the only one of importance enclosing a cheque for a hundred pounds and a note of gratitude for services rendered in a little matter of violence. It was nice to be appreciated.

Jolly said: "Good morning, sir," and Grice's voice came at once: "Is he up?"

"No, sir, but I'm sure he will see you. One moment, sir." There was a pause. "For Mr. Rollison? ... I'll sign." Another pause, murmured courtesies followed, then the door closed, and Grice said in a tone which was only partly flippant: "We'd better make sure that isn't an infernal machine; we don't want you to have more pieces to pick up."

"No doubt Mr. Rollison will attend to that," said Jolly pointedly. He reached the bedroom door, with Grice so well disciplined that he did not come forward at once. "A packet from the Miramar Hotel, sir, delivered by a bell-boy, and Mr. Grice has called."

"I'll take 'em both at once," said Rollison.

Grice came in as Jolly handed Rollison the packet. Grice was smiling faintly, and was obviously still conscious of the terms on which they had parted the night before. Rollison did not welcome him buoyantly, but was not aloof.

"Hallo, Bill. Take a chair. Like some tea or coffee?"

"No, thanks. Who's sent you a present?"

Rollison didn't answer, but felt the packet, which yielded very slightly. He held it to his ear, shook it, then handed it to Grice. Jolly stood in the doorway. All three had mental flashbacks; to the time when Grice had been examining something like this, and it had exploded into his face. Death had been very close.

It could happen again.

"Bath-tub?" asked Rollison, calmly.

"Feels all right," Grice said. "Let's be careful with it. You going to open it, or shall I?"

"I will," said Rollison. He got out of bed and took the packet to a small table by the window. "Tell me things while I'm doing it, I need balm for my nerves. Those tablets?"

"Arsenic in the stomach tablets, which had been impregnated," said Grice. "The couple we caught there yesterday could have done that. Arsenic in McGinn's stomach, but not much—although if the doctor hadn't been quick the patient would have had a very bad time."

Rollison was slitting the gummed paper with which the packet was sealed, using a thin-bladed knife and working very carefully.

"Rory?"

"He came to see me last night and tried to raise hell and hallelujah. But he quietened down, and he's back with his uncle."

Rollison glanced up, stopping his work; the gummed paper was nearly free, now. Jolly still hovered in the background, watching, and it was evident that he feared a repetition of the explosion; and Rollison would have been the last man in the world to say that it wouldn't happen.

"What quietened him?"

"We let him take Miss Daventry back, after we'd questioned her. She went to the Miramar. There's always room for a guest of a millionaire."

"D'you mean you haven't hanged her yet?"

"We haven't hanged Norris yet, either," said Grice, very mildly.

Rollison smiled faintly.

Men were odd creatures, and he was a man. Now he half wished that Bella was safe in custody. But the police would watch her, wouldn't they? They'd make no mistake?

The last piece of gummed paper round the package came free. He opened the outer wrapping, and found more inside. A third sheet of brown paper was beneath that. Rollison took this off with great care, keeping his face averted, ready to fling it aside at any moment.

He didn't have to fling it.

The third wrapper was the last. Inside were many five-pound notes. There were two wads, placed side by side, and the notes looked new, an inch thick or more, black printing on crisp white paper; and there were at least a hundred notes in each pile.

"Good gracious me!" exclaimed Jolly, squeakily.

Grice didn't even squeak.

Rollison picked up a sealed envelope, glanced at Grice, and said in a casual voice: "You'd better resign from the Yard and become a private eye, obviously that's where the money is made." Rollison glanced at Jolly. "Did Mr. McGinn telephone you?"

"No, sir."

"He talked of a thousand-pound retainer, and I thought he was just making an impression," Rollison went on, still casually. He opened the letter, and the single sheet of folded paper, with the crest of the Miramar on it. The letter was typewritten, and signed in brilliant purple ink.

Dear Richard Rollison,
I am a man of my word. And I know you are a man of yours. I send you by special messenger the retainer, and also £100 for today. Because I am in urgent need of your services, which will mean you will have to miss your ball game.

Will you be good enough to come here as near eleven o'clock as you can?

Cordially,
Connor K. McGinn

Chapter Twenty-One

Mr. McGinn In A Hurry

Connor McGinn came forward from the French windows of the big room overlooking Hyde Park. He gripped Rollison's hands tightly. He looked pale and unwell, which wasn't surprising, but his hand-clasp was firm if his voice was a little husky.

"You're good to come, Rollison. I guess I know how you feel about that ball game. But we can have the radio on, you don't have to miss it all." His smile was a little too broad. "I want to tell you what I've decided, and I don't think you'll blame me for it, I really don't. I'm going to finish my business here in a hurry, and get right back to the United States. I confess I don't like the things that have been happening, and after that poison—well, sir, I just don't feel safe here. I can't imagine who would want to kill me, but it is apparent that someone does." He forced the big smile again. "That means Europe isn't so healthy for me."

Rollison said: "Trouble could follow you around."

"If I'm heading for trouble I'd rather meet up with it in my own country," said McGinn. "Not that I think it will follow me around. No, sir! But I'm wasting time here, and that won't do. I'm having a big day right here in this room, Mr. Rollison. I'm buying what jewels I can examine today, and I'm writing the rest off. The jewels I had here yesterday are in the bank vaults. Dealers are coming to see me today—I've been in touch with some of them, and Rory and that

Bella Daventry have been very helpful. I just have to say that for them."

"How?"

"They've been telephoning other dealers and telling them what kind of gems I want to see here," explained McGinn, "and they both know enough to be sure that they're asking for the right stones. The first dealer is due at half-past eleven."

It was then five minutes past the hour.

"Have you told Grice about this?"

"I didn't tell Grice, because he wasn't in his office, but I told someone else at Scotland Yard," said McGinn. "I am not taking any chances at all, Mr. Rollison. After what happened here yesterday, I'd be crazy to take even one. You want to hear what I've done? The hotel detectives have been alerted. Three of the Yard's C.I.D. officers are here, and more are on the way. That's for outside the room. Inside the room, there will be just three of us, and one dealer at a time, possibly two but never *more* than two, representatives of the same firm. There'll be you, Rory and"—he gave a little chuckle— "Connor McGinn! We shall all be armed. I just can't believe that in view of ail the precautions anything will go wrong, but I tell you I'm taking no chances at all. You agree that I'm wise?"

"I couldn't agree more. Where will Miss Daventry be?"

"I don't need telling why you put that question," said McGinn. "You are asking yourself whether it was wise for me to allow a partner of a man known to be a crook to realise what was going on. You're wondering, like me, if Bella has got in touch with this Arthur Rowe, whom the police want to find, and told him. Well, it's anybody's guess, but don't say that to Rory. No, sir, it wouldn't be wise." McGinn's eyes held a glint of a smile. "He's mad at you already, don't make him any madder. I think he might overcome his inhibitions, then, and step right out of this fear of being hurt! It's surprising what a lovely girl can do to a man."

Rollison said: "Yes." He lit a cigarette, watching the millionaire closely. "What do you think of her, yourself?"

"We still haven't yet met," said McGinn. "I got up late this morning, and she and Rory had breakfast together. Then they did this telephoning for me, and now they've gone out for a walk. I saw them from the window, and Bella looks swell, but—" His eyes were suddenly very direct, very wide open. "Do *you* trust her?"

Rollison said: "I think so. I want to."

McGinn relaxed.

"Rory tells me that he just can't believe that she would do anything wrong." He chuckled, but suddenly became very grave again. "I sure hope he's right. I hope *I'm* right. Those two young folk, the police, the dealers and you and I are the only people who know about the jewels coming here. All the telephone calls were made on lines kept open for us by the telephone engineers. If the information leaks out, then one of them will have talked. Do you agree?"

After a long pause, Rollison said: "Are you telling me that you don't trust your nephew?"

"I'm telling you that I don't know whether to trust that girl, and that I can see that she can do whatever she likes with Rory," McGinn answered grimly. "It was my suggestion that one of the police should follow them. If they do anything peculiar, we'll be informed. I just can't believe—"

There was a movement at the door, and Rory McGinn came in. He nodded frostily to Rollison; whatever his uncle had decided, he wasn't going to be friendly.

"Why, Rory, where's the young lady?" McGinn asked brightly.

"She's gone to her office," Rory told him. "I tried to persuade her to come and rest at the hotel, but she wouldn't, because we'll be so busy. I don't blame her. She'll do better trying to sort out the mess that her company is in. The policeman you sent after us is watching the office," he added, and his voice was bitter.

Connor McGinn said: "All right, boy, all right. Only a fool would be careless. I'm not saying anything against the girl." He glanced at his watch. "Ah, twenty-five after eleven. In five minutes the first dealer should be here—and your ball game starts, Rollison, doesn't it?"

"We don't get it on radio or television yet," Rollison said, straight-faced.

"You don't? Why, that's too bad. Whenever you want to switch on, just say the word." McGinn hesitated, looked at Rory as if he were going to comment on his glowering expression, then changed his mind, for there was a ring at the bell.

"That's the beginning," he said.

McGinn seemed to change before Rollison's eyes when the first dealer came in – Hinniver of Hatton Garden and renowned in every capital city. He was a disreputable-looking little man with sharp features, and outwardly seemed more suitable for a jail than one of the most famous jewellers in the world. He carried two jewel cases in the big, sagging pockets of an old brown coat, and appeared not to have the slightest anxiety about them; or to take any precautions.

McGinn sat at a table near the window, with a special jewellers' light on an Angle-poise frame and a watchmaker's glass available, as well as tiny scales of great precision. He was in his shirt-sleeves. He said very little, but examined the jewels, handling them with tiny forceps, weighing them, occasionally checking with entries in a thin, black-bound book.

He bought one set of diamonds from Hinniver, who left them in the case with him. McGinn wouldn't open an account, and insisted on giving him a cheque for nine thousand pounds. The cheques were already signed, and an account had been opened at a nearby bank. Rory made out the amount and the payee's name, in a sprawling hand.

When Hinniver had gone, McGinn relaxed, but he was still more the connoisseur of precious stones than the steel magnate.

"Know why I bought that set?" he asked. "Come and see for yourselves. I'm making a collection of diamonds from the smallest weight and size Indian and African stones, to the largest I can find. Can't get the Koh-i-noor, I know, but I've one almost as large! Now this set fits in exactly here." He turned over the pages of the book, showing illustrations of his collection, beautiful photographs which gave some idea of the loveliness of the jewels. "Now I've a straight run of weights and sizes from the smallest up to the middle size. Two more sets of diamonds, and they'll be complete. Then I'll stop." He shrugged his shoulders, and gave an unexpectedly boyish smile. "Perhaps," he added, "perhaps."

The next dealer called …

At half-past twelve, Rollison put on the television. He spent five minutes at it, and came away hopeful that the day would go well. He saw pictures of the shirt-sleeved crowd intent and as hopeful as he, and, when the score-board was thrown on to the screen, looked eagerly for Ebbutt and believed that he caught sight of him.

Another dealer came before lunch. Then there was an hour's break for a light luncheon. Rory went off to make a telephone call before the buying started again.

It was a day of jewels, cheques, brisk speech and slow batting, wickets falling suddenly and disastrously, hopes rising sharply, then falling and falling lower; and finally, a day when England was still in the game but only just, forty runs behind with three wickets to fall, and none of these a batsman except the inexorable Mr. Bailey.

Between the wickets, McGinn bought emeralds, rubies, sapphires, diamonds, single stones, small sets, graded stones, stones with unusual histories or with unusual qualities. Here were rose-tinted diamonds, or diamonds which seemed to hold the colour of Bella Daventry's eyes, stones whose history was drenched in blood as awfully as any Roman emperor's.

McGinn was a revelation.

He kept a precise record not only of what stones he bought, but what, he had been offered. He wrote details of everything down on loose-leaf pages which fitted into the back of his stock book, he was almost cold-blooded about it all. Rory filled in the counterfoils of the cheques with great care, and each man added each item to a cumulative total. Every now and again, they checked their figures. McGinn could say exactly how much money he had spent after every transaction. He spent in thousands of pounds where another man might have spent cautiously in tens. There seemed no limit to the total he was prepared to spend, and he seldom haggled; but occasionally he valued a stone differently from a dealer, and made an offer.

Every offer was accepted.

At a quarter to seven, looking tired, haggard and yet oddly satisfied, he yawned and stood up from the table. He had made his last purchase and last entry.

"Rory, mix me an old-fashioned, boy, will you? And you have what you feel like, Rollison." His voice was hoarse. "I'm grateful for you standing by the way you have, I've been able to concentrate on the job. Mind you, I don't like buying this way, I like to spend a day or so over one purchase, you get more fun that way. But I want to get back home! You looking forward to going home, Rory?"

Rory said: "I'm not so sure I'm going with you after all, uncle." His chin jutted out, he looked as if he were ready to argue aggressively.

McGinn gave him a straight look, shrugged, and didn't comment. He took the old-fashioned without a word. Rollison had a whisky-and-soda. He was flat and disappointed for two reasons. He felt that the England score should have been much higher, and the lost wickets fewer; and he had wasted his time here. Nothing had happened, except that he had seen how casual a millionaire could be about his millions. Even the steady spending of money had lost its fascination after the early deals. When McGinn had spent his first twenty thousand, it had seemed a fantastic sum to spend on a few pieces of sparkling stone. When the total was over a hundred and fifty thousand, it had got so past satiation point that it was hardly worth a thought.

And nothing had happened, it had been one of the dullest days of Rollison's life.

It was even difficult to convince himself that there had ever been a risk; that there still was.

Bella had gone to her office; and there was no reason why she shouldn't. She had probably returned to Rye Street by now. The police had let her go, remember, which suggested that Grice had been satisfied with the story after all.

Did it?

Grice was a great believer in dangling sprats to catch mackerels. Grice was good, too, and in on the ground floor of everything. Annoyance with what had happened could be forgotten. As Rollison sipped his drink, he wished that he could see Grice, wanted to get away as soon as he could. Perhaps Grice was free for dinner.

Perhaps Bella was free for dinner.

He scoffed at himself. He could see that Connor McGinn was tired, and Rory seemed tearing at a leash to get away. That wasn't surprising.

Rory telephoned Rye Street, suddenly, asking for Bella. Watching his face, hearing his voice, Rollison felt the first little twinge of anxiety.

"... so she isn't there," Rory said, and then looked startled. "What's that? ... She hasn't been there all day ... Well, I understand— but never mind that, ma'am, if she returns just tell her that Rory McGinn called, will you? ... Rory ... R-O-R-Y. Thank you, ma'am."

He rang off.

He said almost to himself: "But she reckoned she would spend the afternoon at Rye Street."

Rollison said sharply: "Let's call her office."

There was no answer from 217g Hatton Garden.

The beginning of deep alarm stirred in Rollison, and it seemed to rise in Rory, too. The older McGinn was too tired to be greatly affected; he seemed lost in contemplation of the jewels and the day's labours.

Rollison and Rory were by the telephone, Rory's hostility and aloofness gone for the first time that day, apparently swallowed up in bewilderment and anxiety.

"I just don't get it," he said again and again.

"Grice may have picked her up again," Rollison said savagely, and dialled Whitehall 1212.

The Yard answered quickly, but Grice wasn't there.

"He's on the way to the Hotel Miramar," a sergeant said. "I should wait for him, Mr. Rollison. He's been making arrangements to have those jewels watched for the night. Will you wait?"

"Yes. Perhaps you can tell me this: has Miss Daventry been picked up again?"

"Why, no," the sergeant said, "we can't find her. Didn't Mr. Grice tell you?"

Chapter Twenty-Two

The Disappearance Of Bella Daventry

Grice came in, with a Yard man watching closely from the passage; no apartment in London had been guarded with greater care since a Marshal from the Balkans had come on a visit of great goodwill, angering many who disapproved of him.

The door closed.

First Rollison, then Rory, moved towards Grice, who didn't look reassuring. Rory's eyes held a snap, his hands were half-clenched. Rollison bit on his first searing question, and allowed Rory to get in first.

"What's happened to Miss Daventry? I thought you cops were taking care of her. My God, if anything goes wrong with her you'll hear about it!"

He was glaring, his jaw was thrust forward, his fists were tightly clenched. He didn't know Grice as Rollison did, and so couldn't read the signs. Grice just looked at him, and Rory went on in that quivering voice: "Why don't you talk? You were supposed to be taking care of that girl, weren't you? Police? You make me sick!"

"Just at the moment," Grice said, very calmly, "I am not interested in knowing whether you feel well or whether you feel ill. If you want to oblige me, you can get out of the room or you can shut up."

Rory said viciously: "That's no way to talk to me. I can report—"

"That's just fine," said Grice, and smiled very thinly, "that's exactly what I was waiting for. Listen, McGinn, I'm sick to death of having you running round your Embassy and needling them so that they send frantic messages to the Home Office. I'm sick to death of being pushed around, and having to change my own way of working to suit a blown-up apology for an American. Understand? I've taken all I can take, and I'm stopping now. If you hadn't gone belly-aching to friends at the Embassy last night, I'd have held Bella Daventry until I knew she was safe. But you managed to pull strings, and I hadn't a hard-and-fast case, so she had to go. Who are you going to blame? Me? The American Ambassador? Rollison? Or yourself? Take it from me, if anything happens to Miss Daventry, the fault will be yours. And I'll make sure the world knows it!"

He stopped, breathing heavily.

Rory McGinn seemed to crumple. "Now, listen, I wasn't to know——

Grice turned away, ignoring him completely.

"Rolly," Grice said, "Miss Daventry was seen to make a call from a telephone box when she left her office about one-thirty. It didn't take her long. She left the box and caught a bus. Our man ran after her, and was tripped up—deliberately he thinks. Miss Daventry might have known about it—and might not. She didn't turn up at her office or flat. I had a general call put out for her at once, but nothing's come in. We haven't found a trace of Rowe, either. Miss Daventry may have gone to him, or she may have run into trouble. The last man to see her at close quarters was young McGinn, who saw her to Fingleton and Company's office and then came back here." He turned on Rory. "Did Miss Daventry tell you where she was going after leaving the office?"

Rory said: "Sure. Rye Street."

"Well, she didn't turn up, and she certainly gave us the slip," Grice asserted. "I hope to heaven she's all right."

"Why shouldn't she be?" Rory seemed to have lost the courage which rage had given him, and clutched at straws.

"Use your mind," Grice growled, and rubbed his bony chin. "Where's your uncle?"

"Resting."

"The jewels?"

"Right here. We've had a safe brought in, they'll be all right."

"I'm having every door guarded, the windows watched, all the hotel staff on the *qui vive*. If anything happens to those jewels," Grice went on, "it'll be a miracle. Will you tell Mr. McGinn what I'm doing?"

"Sure. Oh, sure," Rory said huskily.

"Coming?" Grice asked Rollison.

They stood outside the Miramar, watched by two splendidly uniformed commissionaires, five newspaper reporters and a number of knowledgeable passers-by. A Yard man was bringing Grice's car up to the end of the covered way outside the hotel.

"All facts?" asked Rollison. "She's missing."

"Just vanished."

"Think she telephoned Rowe?"

"It wouldn't surprise me." Grice's car came up. "Take you anywhere?"

"No, thanks, my car's parked near."

"All right." Grice looked Rollison straight in the eyes. "Is this another Sir Galahad's job?"

"Don't be a ruddy fool," said Rollison.

Grice said slowly: "Rory McGinn and you. She could be very bad, Rolly. She could be just as bad as she looks good." He didn't smile. "I don't say she is, but if she gets in touch with you, be careful. Be *very* careful." Rollison smiled, but wasn't amused.

"Bill."

"Yes."

"Watching Rory McGinn?"

"What?"

"I'm asking."

"Listen," Grice said, "I don't like him, he's a nervous wreck, he's a spoilt pup, he—"

"That's right. He bellyached at the Embassy until you let Bella go. If someone has kidnapped her, the someone would want her out of jail. Rory could have worked for that. Rory could have freed Norris from my flat the other night. I knocked him out at Soho because I didn't trust him. I still don't. Try to find out if he had a telephone call from Bella about the time she used that telephone."

"I'll fix it by radio," Grice snapped.

He got into his car, picking up his walkie-talkie radio, and it slid into the Park Lane traffic. Newspapermen came hopefully towards the Toff. He smiled at them almost blankly, and they let him walk away unquestioned. He kept seeing those sapphire-blue eyes. If Bella were involved, what was she doing? What was the racket? Why had McGinn been kidnapped, poisoned, virtually driven out of the country? That was what it amounted to; he had been hounded out, and couldn't be blamed for going.

Who would want him to go, and why?

Rollison reached his car. He could guess all night and all next day, without getting the right answer. He took the wheel. He almost forgot the Test, the crowds now merging with London's millions, the deserted Oval, the score-boards telling their tale – which would live until morning, when Bailey and Lock would take it up again, and England would begin the long, slow climb towards Australia's two hundred and seventy-five.

What were the inexplicable things?

The disappearance of Rowe. The disappearance of Bella Daventry. The kidnapping and the poisoning of Connor McGinn. The behaviour of Rory. Was Rory bad? Broke? In trouble? He was vice-president and heir to a huge corporation, a millionaire in the making. But he was living on his nerves? Grice would probe, now.

What about the little things? Jeremiah Fingleton hurrying to the Oval, being run down – *little*? The sky clouded over, the night was as depressing as Rollison's thoughts. If it rained, the wicket would be soaked. Well, Lock and Laker might spin the Aussies out, but never mind cricket. Sacrilege! Why had Fingleton gone to the Oval, and – perhaps more important – why had Paul Wrightson followed, and sent that van careering into his co-director with intent to injure and probably intent to kill? Why had they wanted to keep Fingleton away from the match? To stop him from seeing the Toff?

Nonsense!

Another thing about the Oval, too – why had Lemaitre been there that day, as well as Black Norris? Cricket fans came from unexpected places, but would men of the calibre of Black Norris go there for the love of the game on such a day? Arthur Rowe would, according to Bella. Yet Black Norris and Lemaitre had been—

He jerked his head up.

He started the engine, drove out of the parking site, and was at Scotland Yard within five minutes. He didn't go straight up to Grice's office, but called him from a telephone at the reception desk, watched by an elderly, benevolent-looking sergeant who wore a uniform but no hat.

"Bill?"

"Hallo, Rolly. I've just learned one thing. A woman phoned Rory at lunch-time today, but no one knows who it was."

"Pity. Bill, changing the subject. That pair you caught at the Miramar, the man and his Liz."

"'Well?"

"Anything found on them or at their flat to show that they'd been to the Oval?"

After a pause, Grice said slowly: "I haven't noticed anything, but I'll check. Come up, I may have it by the time you get here."

"Right," said Rollison.

It took him almost as long to reach Grice's office as it had to get to Scotland Yard. He tapped and opened the door, and found Grice standing up, scanning a typewritten list, with a plain-clothes man by him.

" 'Evening, sir."

"Hallo," said Rollison, and went to Grice's side. "Any luck?"

"Test Match score-card," Grice read, almost explosively. "Found in the waste-paper box at Miller's flat. Details of Saturday's play filled in until the fall of Hassett's wicket." Grice's eyes blazed at the plain-clothes man. "Get that card."

"Yes, sir!" The man fled.

"Now we're moving, I think," said Rollison, making himself speak slowly. His heart was beating very fast. "I pray. We want Rowe. Fingleton was going to the Oval, Norris, Lemaitre, Miller and maybe others in this racket were there. Lemaitre and Miller said they'd had orders from Arthur Rowe, but wouldn't say where they'd seen him. Well, why not at the Oval? They all left at about the same time, between the fall of Hassett's wicket and the one after it. I forgot who it was, but it didn't take long."

The plain-clothes man came back.

"The last entry on Miller's card is the fall of the third wicket, sir," he confirmed.

"Bill," breathed Rollison, "let's see Miller, let's find out if he saw Rowe there. Trick questions should do it. And let me—"

"All right," Grice said. "Come on."

Miller did not look so buoyant as he had at the Miramar, and judging from the dark patches under his eyes, he hadn't slept much. But he wasn't cowed, and he sneered at Roilison when he was brought in.

"What method are you going to use this time?" he demanded. "Mind reading?"

Rollison said: "All right, Miller, be clever." No yorker had ever started more innocently. "What time did you leave Rowe at the Oval on Saturday?"

The crook's good-looking face twisted in utter stupefaction. He gaped, gasped, tried to recover, and then gave way, as if he had been punctured.

He had met Rowe at the Oval, and received his orders there. He always got orders there – from Rowe or Norris, in the summer. In winter they used football grounds and dog- and dirt-track stadiums. He didn't know who else had been there; although he had seen Norris. There may have been others of the gang. They had met near the gasometer score-board, the usual spot. Had they got away with the jewels, they would probably have had a message to go to the same place on Monday.

Bella Daventry hadn't been in the ground. Miller knew her slightly, but she didn't know what he did for a living. He did not know of any plot except to rob Connor McGinn of his jewels. He had never heard Rory McGinn mentioned; but then Rowe seldom mentioned others and talked very little. The only impression Rowe had left was that this was to be a big coup; he had been quite sure that he would fool the police.

"And he didn't say how?" Grice broke in.

"Not a word," Miller muttered. "There isn't a thing more I can say."

"Have you a photograph of Rowe?" Grice demanded.

"No," Miller said, "Never seen one, either, he was shy, you never knew what he'd turn up in next. Dressed different, looked different every time."

Grice sent him away.

"If we'd only a photograph," he groaned, as they went back to his office. "Until we know what he looks like—"

"Anything about Jenkinson, from South Africa?"

"Not a thing," Grice said, and went into his office.

A radio telegram and a telephoto picture of a man named Jenkinson, once sentenced to eight years imprisonment for robbery with violence, lay on his desk.

He whipped it down to Miller.

"Could be Rowe," Miller said. "He's a lot fatter than that now. But yes—it could be."

"Nice job," Grice growled. "In the morning we'll search the Oval crowd for Arthur Rowe, alias Jenkinson. We've only an old photograph and a vague description. But I'll get hundreds of copies of the photograph printed, every man on duty at the Oval will have one."

"I'll get Brian Castor to co-operate, too," Rollison said. "He will, like a shot. Have all the stewards, officials, ice-cream sellers, bar attendants, every man jack of them with a picture of Rowe."

Unexpectedly, Grice grinned.

"What part of the ground will you search?" he demanded.

"I'll leave Arthur Rowe to you," Rollison said, without a vestige of a smile. "I'll be looking for Bella Daventry. You keep an eye on Rory McGinn, Bill. And Connor, too. Don't let anything happen to him. We couldn't face the consequences."

"Until he's out of the country we'll watch him and his jewels every minute," Grice said. "And Rory's being followed, everywhere he goes."

"That's fine," Rollison said.

When he reached home, he telephoned Bill Ebbutt, who was up, and reported that his lump was considerably smaller.

"That's fine," Rollison said. "So you'll be at the Oval tomorrow?"

"Even if I go by 'earse, Mr. Ar."

"Fine, Bill. Get as near the gasometer score-board as you can tomorrow, will you?"

"Take it from me we will, was there today," Ebbutt said. "Why?"

"Have some of the boys with you, and keep a look out for me," Rollison urged.

"Still arter that six?" demanded Ebbutt, then suddenly guffawed.

Chapter Twenty-Three

The Second Disappearance Of Connor McGinn

It was eight o'clock when Rollison woke next morning; his normal time. Jolly was bringing in tea, newspapers and the post. Outside, the sky looked grey, and Rollison peered anxiously out of the window.

"It's brighter than it was, sir," said Jolly, "and the forecast is reasonably satisfactory. The newspapers are rather dejected about our prospects this morning."

"So am I. Nothing from Grice?"

"No message of any kind, sir, since he told us that Ebbutt has those photographs of Rowe. The newspapers have an account of Miss Daventry's disappearance."

He poured out tea.

Rollison opened a newspaper, and saw Bella's face peering out. He didn't know where the photograph had been obtained, but it was good; and half England would pause in its anxious hopes for the day's play and the task of Bailey, Lock, Bedser and Trueman, who would go questing dourly for forty-odd needed runs. But few would look at Bella's beauty as intently as the Toff.

He put the paper aside.

"It isn't time for a parcel of fivers, is it?" he asked, in a tone which failed woefully to be lighthearted.

"I'll run your bath, sir," said Jolly.

At nine, Grice telephoned; there was no fresh news, except that Lemaitre had also admitted that he had seen Arthur Rowe at the Oval. No word had come in from the Divisions or the Home Counties about Bella Daventry.

"Connor McGinn is leaving the country today," Grice said, "but Rory has cancelled his passage by BOAC, ostensibly to wait until Bella Daventry turns up. He's just prowled around."

"What time is Connor McGinn leaving?"

"Ten o'clock, from the hotel, eleven fifteen from London airport."

"I'll go and see him at the hotel. Protect him as you would your life, or even me," pleaded Rollison. " 'Bye." He rang off, and went very thoughtfully to his breakfast, which Jolly was putting on the dining-alcove table. He looked up into Jolly's lined face, and said quietly: "Grice believes that she's working with Rowe, and that they'll go off together. Do you?"

"I don't know her well enough, sir," said Jolly, judicially, "but you certainly gave me the impression that she is devoted to this Arthur Rowe. She might be of the temperament to make great sacrifices for a man to whom she believes she owes a great deal."

Rollison grunted, "Maybe," and went on with his breakfast.

Outside, London was stirring to a strange day. Every man worthy of the name had read every word he could find about the previous day's play; and studied all forecasts for today. Few people's were cheerful. A jubilant kangaroo seemed to leap across the printed pages, even across the face of Bella Daventry.

Outside the Oval, a crowd of quiet, orderly people moved slowly towards the entrance gates, just as they had the day before, although with many more anxious glances at the sky. But the clouds, though massed and massive, gradually seemed to rise higher; and over to the north-west the sun shone.

Inside, Bill Ebbutt and his men were already settled near the score-board.

Every official, every seller of match cards, every policeman, everyone who could be called upon had that photograph in his pocket and studied it occasionally, sometimes boldly, more often furtively; and stared in the faces of strangers, wondered, compared and shook their heads.

Reports that Arthur Rowe had been seen started to come in at half-past ten, and twenty-nine reached Grice, at the secretary's office, by half-past eleven. Only two of the men brought in were even remotely like the photograph.

Play began.

Rollison, having wished McGinn well, and spoken to those who were to follow him and his fortune to the airport, was in his place at eleven twenty-nine. He had a perfect view of the first sharp shock to England's hopes, when Lock went, another Lindwall victim, and the applause which followed him to the pavilion was subdued and worried. It was getting hot, the sun was more often out than in, shirt-sleeves replaced raincoats, knotted handkerchiefs sprang up like mushrooms as caps or hats.

Trueman came busily in and showed no sign of nerves. Every run was cheered as if it were a century.

Bailey's slim, dark-haired form looked as if it was part of the field.

Trueman hit a four.

Rollison studied all the people in the stand above him, using his glasses, looking, longing.

He heard footsteps just alongside, then a touch on his shoulder, and turned to see the fair-haired young official who had once brought Bella Daventry to him. This time, he was alone. Members near the Toff frowned, for this distracted from the only thing that mattered; the game.

"Mr. Grice would like a word with you, sir."

Rollison thought: "They've got him!" If they had Rowe, there was a chance that they would have Bella. He got up as the crowd cheered a single which had come off Trueman's edge. The restful scene of white-clad men on rain-washed green faded as Rollison turned, looked perforce into a sea of intent and serious faces, then reached the big room, and hurried towards the office. His heart was thumping.

Grice was standing in the secretary's office, with two other Yard men.

"Got him?" Rollison asked, almost fiercely.

"No," said Grice, and killed jubilation. Now it was evident that he looked badly shaken. "McGinn's disappeared again."

The statement was laconic and emphatic, but didn't really make any sense. The Yard men looked as shaken as their boss. Some stroke or piece of fielding brought a burst of applause from outside, but Rollison hardly noticed it.

"No," he said. It was unbelievable. "No, Bill. You're fooling."

"He's gone."

"But I saw him myself. Spoke to your men, too." This was like a savage blow.

"He left the hotel at five-past ten, and a chauffeur – from his London office, a man we screened thoroughly – drove him to the London airport in the blue Cadillac. We had a car in front, another behind. Police patrols along the route were alerted. McGinn had the jewels with him, and he also had a gun; so did his chauffer. He was trailed closely as far as the road junctions at the end of the double carriageway on the Great West Road. Then he went towards Staines, away from the airport. The Cadillac was found, smashed up in a lane. No one saw what car McGinn changed into, no one knows what happened. Our front car was fooled, the one we had following McGinn was forced off the road by a motor-cyclist. They're brilliant." Grice spoke as if he were forcing every word out. "Well, there it is. He's been snatched with nearly three hundred thousand pounds' worth of jewels. And there isn't a sign of Arthur Rowe or Bella Daventry. I'm beginning to think—" He paused.

Rollison said savagely: "Yes, I know. You're beginning to think that the Oval talk was a blind, the score-cards were blinds. Bill, *think*. If the cards had been blank, or if they'd been nicely and neatly filled in, yes, I—*what's that?*"

A mighty gasp from thirty thousand throats found its way into the office, and every eye turned towards the window. One Yard man went towards it, as if pulled by unseen strings.

"Trueman's out," he called.

"What's the score?" asked Rollison, mechanically.

"Two sixty-one, I think. Can't quite see."

"I'm going to see that Cadillac myself," Grice said. "Care to come?"

"There's Bedser," a Yard man said from the window, and never had the magnetism of this game for flannelled fools been more strongly felt. "He's done pretty well with the bat sometimes. Only want about fifteen to pass 'em. If—"

Rollison said: "Yes, I'll come."

The car had been removed from the lane, and was at Scotland Yard when Grice and Rollison arrived. Rollison had said very little, Grice practically nothing. Different thoughts had chased one another through Rollison's mind, and all the time fear for Bella – and fear that he was wrong about Bella – had been uppermost.

Now, he was fighting to answer inexplicable things. So was Grice.

"It's just flattened me," said Grice. "How on earth did McGinn come to be so easily fooled? He was driven by a man he trusted. He wouldn't have a stranger in the car, which was understandable. He was sitting in the back, with a strong-box on the floor by his feet, and then the Cadillac had swept up to ninety miles an hour. How—?"

"There it is," Grice said a little later, getting out of his Morris. "Lovely job, before it was piled up."

The sky-blue Cadillac was shimmering in the bright sunshine, and Rollison remembered looking down on it from the window of Paul Wrightson's flat. Three days ago? It seemed an age. There it was sleek, plump, shining, beautiful, except on one side; as different from his own Rolls-Bentley as a car could be, yet not unworthy of comparison.

Two men were leaning inside, tight-clad, rounded rumps showing, one man sweeping, the other testing different surfaces for prints. The pieces of paper and oddments were brushed carefully into a dustpan. The man who was sweeping drew out, flushed to his forehead, and jolted his elbow against the door; some of the dust and pieces of paper fell out.

"Sorry, sir," he said to Grice.

"All right."

Grice and Rollison looked down at oddments; toffee papers, cardboard matches with blackened heads, a book of matches marked BOAC, some odd pieces of white paper with black printing on it.

One piece caught Rollison's eye. He plucked it out of the fluff and the dust. Grice, seeing his quickening interest, looked down at it. It said:*"… alia, 1st Innings."*

"These pieces!" exclaimed Rollison. "Get 'em together, quick. It looks like another score-card—"

"But McGinn wasn't at the Oval," protested Grice, "he doesn't know a bat from a bail!"

"Piece it together," cried the Toff, and looked as if a blinding light were dazzling him. "Bill—supposing McGinn *wanted* to escape. Supposing he was in league with the chauffeur, that it is all a colossal hoax, a great impersonation. Supposing the man we know as McGinn is really *Arthur Rowe.*"

Grice said in a strangled voice: "No, you're crazy."

The blinding light still shone against Rollison's eyes.

"We're both crazy! Rory draws our fire, reeks suspicion, throws up the genuine character of Uncle Connor. Uncle Connor himself gets snatched, vanishes, and then we get an anonymous note saying where we'll find him—to make sure we do. Then Rory accepts him, that makes him one hundred per cent genuine to the gullible police and the gullible private eye. And Bella, who knows Rowe, must not be allowed to see him. She—"

He almost choked.

Grice just stood piecing the torn pieces. "Filled in to lunch-time," he said.

"One glimpse of the false McGinn and Bella could have thrown an outsize spanner," Rollison went on, "but don't make it obvious, let her go to a dinner-party, then have Rowe-McGinn poisoned and put out of action—a self-made victim of arsenic tablets too weak to do him any harm."

"Let's get to the Oval," Grice rasped. "If McGinn is there—" He stepped to his car, then stopped. "Sergeant!"

"Yes, sir?"

The man with dustpan and brush jumped.

"Go upstairs, have this message put out to all officers looking for Arthur Rowe. Height, five feet eleven, weight about sixteen stone, smooth skin, plump face, light-grey eyes, full lips, grey hair, fair eyebrows and lashes—got all that?"

"Yes, sir."

"Add a message to anyone who's seen Connor McGinn in London. McGinn and Rowe might be one and the same person."

"Right, sir."

"Hurry. Come on, Rolly." Grice was thrusting open the door of his car.

"Now I know the Yard can move fast," Rollison said, and got in. He still looked dazzled, and started to talk before Grice had the engine going. "Bill, Bill, the man has genius, if he weren't a killer I'd take off my hat to him. He turns the spotlight on himself, and with Rory's help, Rory the skunk's help, he fools us. He stages a kidnapping, says the crooks were after his sparklers. He stages a burglary at the Miramar, which didn't work because Grice was too quick. Liz and Miller probably didn't know it, but Rowe-McGinn sacrificed that pair, he always knew they'd never get away. Why?"

Grice was speeding round Parliament Square.

"Go on."

"Simply to draw attention to his jewels. McGinn as a victim of calculated robbery, McGinn so fed up and scared that he's going to go home, but obstinately determined to buy the jewels he's come for. Oh, Bill."

They were in Victoria Street.

"It's fiendishly cunning."

"And so simple. Look at the by-play, too. Knowing the real McGinn's been talking to me, he follows up when he's 'rescued'. I'd have made it clear if I suspected him by then. Rory could be sure I didn't. So play me up, make me the greatest private eye in Europe, throw a casual thousand quid to show how desperately he wants me to save his jewels. I don't think I've ever—"

He choked again; this time on a cigarette he didn't realise that he'd lit.

They were swinging along Vauxhall Bridge Road, the Oval wasn't far away now. Grice drove more as if he were at Donnington Park than a London thoroughfare.

"—met his like. All London jewellers were fooled. He'd the signed cheques—oh Bill, it gets more dazzling. He kidnapped the real McGinn, made him sign those cheques, and then—"

This time Rollison stopped because of dark, menacing thoughts which dimmed the blinding light. Was the real McGinn alive? Was Bella?

There was no proof, but in his heart he was quite sure that he was right, that this was a fabulous impersonation.

They swung beneath the railway arches beyond Vauxhall Bridge.

"Look at the photograph," Grice said.

Rollison gulped. "There's routine for you." He took out the picture, studied it, held a hand over the lower part of the face, and said: "The same eyes and forehead. He's much fatter, his nose has been altered, I should say he's had plastic surgery at the corners of his lips, too. But now we know, we can see the likeness."

"Unless you are crazy," Grice said.

He was stopped by traffic within sight of the Oval's brick wall. A newsboy shouted: *"Lunch score, Test latest."*

"Rory might talk, if we get him," Rollison said. "Rory must talk. He—"

Grice shot him a quick, searching glance.

"He what?"

"He wouldn't kill Bella, would he? He really loves her. Doesn't he?" The questions shot out fiercely.

Grice didn't answer; the lights changed, and he went on.

Atop the Oval walls were heads; a myriad heads, dark, fair and bald or topped with hats, caps, handkerchiefs, paper. On top of every building in sight were people sitting, squatting, standing. At every window sat men and women and children. On the tops of buses, every eye was turned towards the ground. Conductors stood on the top desk, shouting the score to passengers below. Something for one. The flags at the gasometers fluttered. People thronged the streets outside, asking eager questions, and as Rollison and Grice turned round by the Oval Station, there came a loud roar from the crowd.

"Someone's out!" exclaimed a man, passing by.

"That's two!" another cried jubilantly.

"I think—" began Rolhson.

He stopped speaking, for he saw a man hurrying along the pavement towards the turnstiles and the main gates, close to the spot where Jeremiah Fingleton had been killed. It was Rory McGinn.

"Let me out," Rollison snapped, "come yourself, and leave the car. There's Rory."

Grice pulled into the kerb. Rollison opened the door and jumped out. He was going to follow Rory, had no intention yet of letting the man see him, but he dared not lose his quarry.

He saw a uniformed policeman rush up to Grice; Grice would soon be coming.

Something, perhaps he would never know what, made Rory turn his head. Rollison was only three yards behind, and two short people were between them.

Rollison's hand dropped to his pocket and a gun, expecting anything from sudden shots to a wild dash. Neither happened. Rory McGinn stood still, then turned round slowly. His lips were working, his eyes glittered, he was sickly pale, obviously a terribly frightened man. There was no pretence about that now.

"Rollison," he muttered. "Rollison, we must—must find Rowe. The—the man you know as my uncle. He's here somewhere, getting rid—getting rid of the jewels. Meeting—meeting contact men. He—he said he'd let Bella and my uncle go free, but now I know he doesn't mean to. He'll kill them. He—he might have killed them already. He's here somewhere, we've got to make—to make him tell us where—"

He couldn't go on.

Grice was just behind Rollison. "I heard," he said, "Come on."

Chapter Twenty-Four

A Six For The Toff

They went through the gates, delayed for precious minutes, Yard men and Divisional men came hurrying when they recognised Grice. He had sent for men from the Yard who had seen and would recognise McGinn *alias* Rowe, but it would be some time before they arrived. Here at the Oval were just three people who would be able to identify the man.

Grice was brisk.

"Mr. McGinn, I'll send two men with you. If you recognise Rowe, don't show it and don't do anything yourself. Just tell my men, they'll see to the rest."

"All—ah right, but hurry!"

Grice said: "Take the Vauxhall end, Sharp, don't get separated from Mr. McGinn."

"Yes, sir."

"Come on!" cried Rory McGinn, and started off too quickly. But the Yard men were on his heels, and wouldn't let him go.

"I'll take the score-board on the other side," said Grice, pointing along the passage-way between the pavilion, the stands and the restaurant on the left. "You go towards the gasometer score-board. Ebbutt's there, isn't he?"

Rollison nodded.

"Follow Mr. Rollison," Grice ordered two more men.

"Yes, sir."

"And you've got to get Rowe alive," Grice said grimly. "Don't make any mistake. He kidnapped that girl, and he kidnapped the real McGinn. If he kills himself we may never find them. Do exactly what Mr. Rollison tells you. All clear?"

"Yes, sir."

"I hope to heaven he's not sitting on the grass," Rollison said. "If I walk round the boundary he'll see me yards away." He was talking almost to himself, as he led the way.

Here was the scene which he had glimpsed the other day, but now there was tension in the air; tension in the faces of every man and woman standing, squatting or sitting and staring into the great oval and the taut, tense players. The ball came smartly off a bat, there was a round of applause, a few high-pitched: "Well fielded." That was all. Rollison went on, and reached the crowded path between the terraces on the right and the wooden seats placed just round the edges of the grass.

It was hot.

People sat twenty deep round the ground on that green grass, all in shirt-sleeves or light dresses, every eye turned towards the wicket. The score-board said 59 for 2. More people stood looking over Rollison's head and the heads of the Yard men widi him. It wasn't easy to push by. Stragglers walked in each direction, always kept turning their heads to see just another ball.

"*Ooooh!*" cried ten thousand people, as a ball whistled past an Australian bat. "That Lock, what a boy," someone else said. "Must have turned a foot."

The sun shone on the fair hair of Mr. Lock of Surrey.

Now and again Rollison glanced at the field and saw the bowling, but he hardly noticed it. The crowd applauded every piece of fielding, nearly every ball. It was hard going. Rollison scanned each fat face he passed, and that took time, for there were so many hundreds jammed into every few yards of the terrace. Nine men to every woman; ninety white faces to every one black; old men, young men, small boys squatting on the wall, fat men—that was his interest, fat men. And to make sure of getting his man, if Rowe *alias*

McGinn were here, he had to see him and turn away in time to leave the arrest to the men of the C.I.D.

Fat men—

There were fat faces by the dozen, sweating, shiny, greasy, each turned towards the green, none of them faintly interested in what was happening on the path. Why should they be? Ice-cream boys passed along, pushing and shoving, not thinking of calling their wares.

A fat man—

"He's out!" came a roar, and suddenly thirty thousand people moved as one, thirty thousand mouths opened, thirty thousand larynxes let forth a mighty roar. "Hole's out!" they cried. "Laker's got him!" Suddenly the still and silent mass became a seething one, men turned to neighbours, shouted, talked, beamed, laughed, slapped unfamiliar backs, clapped hot, damp hands, eased their position, began to talk in undertones of great excitement; and the names of a certain Mr. Laker and of a Mr. Lock were on every tongue.

An Australian walked slowly towards the pitch from the pavilion, and Rollison, knowing it was pointless to carry on his search just then, looked and saw him, and wondered whether this man would be the usual Australian saving strength.

The crowd settled down.

Bella, lovely Bella—

Rollison walked on, scanning every face, especially every fat face, and saw no one he recognised until, not far away from the score-board with its back to the gasometer, he saw the back of a nearly bald head with a strangely conical shape rising up from it.

"Bill," he called, and pushed forward.

There was Bill Ebbutt with all his cronies in seats fit for kings, big men or made tall by rubber cushions, so that they could sit and see everything over the heads of the squatting or kneeling crowd on the grass.

"Bill!"

"Caw, 'ow'd you like it?" wheezed Bill Ebbutt. "Got free of 'em. It's our day, Mr. Ar, I c'n fell it in me bones. That Lock!" 'That Lock' started his short run, .and Ebbutt's voice stopped wheezing and became a mighty roar. "Come on, Lock. Don't let 'im settle dahn."

The crowd near him roared, and he shouted again. Lock bowled, and the ball whipped off the pitch and past the bat, the stumps and the prance of Mr. Evans, but a slip flung himself and grabbed it, and earned applause enough for a brilliant catch or a fine run out.

"Wake things up, Lock!" boomed Bill Ebbutt.

Rollison looked at him from one side and saw his shining face, the tense look in his eyes, the parted lips, the fierce desire in him; and Rollison turned away, leaving him to the glory of his hopes.

Rollison and the two Yard men reached the score-board.

Just behind it, a man moved suddenly, and Rollison caught sight of him, and wondered why he moved. He didn't look towards the spot at once, but strolled on, peering to the right and the left but not behind. Then he turned; and the hunt was over.

Arthur Rowe wore a cycling cap with a big peak, hoping to hide his eyes. He couldn't. His eyelashes and eyebrows were dyed, almost black – too dark. His cheeks were olive instead of very fair, stained with some natural-looking dye. He wore a soiled green shirt, shapeless flannels and big suede shoes, and he carried an ice-cream tray.

He started to walk towards the far end, away from Rollison.

"Man with the khaki cap and the tray," Rollison breathed to the Yard men, and they spotted their man and went swiftly on. One pushed past McGinn *alias* Arthur Rowe. The other kept just behind him, they had only to pounce to get him now.

But fate was hovering; and pounced instead.

"He's Out!" came a roar, a thunderous jubilation touched with unbelief. Two doughty Australian wickets had fallen in a few short minutes. How the crowd roared and cheered and waved and turned a quiet multitude into a seething throng. "Lock, Lock, Lock's the boy!" roared Ebbutt. "Keep awake, Lock boy, don't go to sleep!"

The surging crowd got in the way of detectives and stopped McGinn *alias* Rowe.

He turned, and saw Rollison. Rollison began to hurry, but the pressure of the crowd was too great. Rollison and Rowe were just at the rear of Ebbutt's party, and Ebbutt still roaring.

There was Rowe-McGinn, fat, stained face streaked with dirt, open-neck shirt grubby, peaked cap low over his eyes, knapsack over his shoulder. Suddenly, the ice-cream tray dropped. It fell on a corner, the lid opened, wrapped ice-cream – strawberry, vanilla and chocolate coated – fell out in a colourful stream.

Jewels followed.

Diamonds, rubies, emeralds, sapphires seemed to set the concrete path on fire.

The two Yard men had been pushed to one side, and there was only a few feet between the man and Rollison – Rollison saw the gun leap into a fat hand.

"Look out!" he cried, "look out!"

McGinn *alias* Rowe flourished the gun, trying to get a clear aim at Rollison. People, scared with alarm, swayed to right and left. Ebbutt jumped up, and turned away from the field. Rollison dug out his own gun, but before he fired and before the killer fired, Ebbutt became like an erupting volcano.

He was up on his seat and leaping at the fat Rowe-McGinn, bellowing, terrifying. Rowe-McGinn faltered, and Ebbutt crashed into him.

They went down.

The gun didn't go off.

A few people stared and looked scared, but before Ebbutt was up, with his prisoner helpless in a hammer-lock, and before the Yard men took over, many were, shouting: "Siddown, there."

"Come on, let's see the play."

"If you don't siddown—"

"That cove?" Ebbutt breathed. "Often seen 'im 'ere, Mr. Ar. I noo 'e was passing on summink, lot of bad types; saw 'im reg'lar. 'Oo is 'e?"

"We're going to find out, Bill. Thanks. You stay, we can manage." Other police came up, while spectators picked up pieces of coloured glass and handed them over, a small boy snatched an ice-cream—

Rollison led the way, and two Yard men followed, with their prisoner. Ebbutt, waved away by the Toff, had gone back to his seat. Police were still scrambling for jewels. No one took the slightest notice of the party going towards the pavilion.

Word sped round for Grice and Rory McGinn; before it reached them, Rollison and the police were searching a sullen Rowe's pockets.

"All right, save yourself the trouble," he said. "Bella and McGinn are alive, you'll find them in a house at Isleworth." He sneered. "If Rory hadn't got cold feet, you'd never—"

Rollison said: "What's the address?"

"Five Oaks Avenue, near the station. They're okay, I tell you."

"They'd better be," said Rollison icily.

Soon Grice came hurrying.

As he reached them a roar came from the ground, louder, fiercer, almost savage in its glee. And in that moment, Grice, the Toff and Arthur Rowe looked at each other without thought of murder, rescue, jewels or crime in their minds; each was startled, each unbelieving.

"Not *another*," breathed Rowe. "We're going to beat 'em."

Rollison said to Grice: "Come on, Bill, we want Isleworth, in a hurry."

Bella was tied hand and foot to an armchair, and the real Connor McGinn on the floor, tied to the foot of a single bed.

He looked ill and badly frightened.

Bella was in a state of collapse when Rollison cut her free.

It had started a long time ago, when Rory McGinn had gambled with the steel trust's European funds, lost, taken more to try to recoup, lost again, and found himself in desperate straits.

Among the men he gambled with was Arthur Rowe.

Rowe had given him a little help, to tide him over, and caught him in a web too strong to break.

So Rory had introduced his uncle to Fingleton's, on his first brief visit to England. Paul Wrightson had made the big mistake, selling stolen gems when he should have made sure of winning Connor McGinn's confidence, so that he could be robbed on a big scale. But it was done, and Connor's suspicions had become very lively.

The original plot had been to rob McGinn after his orgy of buying. But he was much too restive, and had made it clear to Rory by telephone that he was going to make trouble when he reached England again.

Rory had begged him to wait, for Bella's sake; to be sure of his facts before going to the police. So Connor had asked for Rollison's help, having heard a great deal about the Toff.

The impersonation plan had really been born then.

Desperate to keep his uncle away from the Toff, Rory had telephoned Rowe, and they had hatched up a story to lure McGinn out of London, planning to have Norris – already laid on as his uncle's driver by Rory – shanghai him. Connor McGinn had elected to drive himself, lost his way (that much of the false McGinn's story had been true) and telephoned the office from a suburb. So Rory had sent Black Norris to take over the car.

Connor McGinn's first call had been on Paul Wrightson's flat, and that hadn't mattered.

Black Norris had dealt with him before he'd got back into the hotel.

By then, Rowe had seen all the possibilities of an impersonation.

By chance, McGinn had arrived at the London airport after dark. Few people had seen him come into the hotel. Rory had signed him in and shown the reception desk his passport. Rory, to curry favour, had fetched and carried for his uncle, and none of the hotel servants had actually set eyes on McGinn in his apartment.

So Rowe had decided to take the big chance. The two men were of the same build, and wearing the real McGinn's clothes he might get by. There was a big risk, but the stakes were fabulously high.

McGinn had been frightened into signing the cheques, and the whole plot was quickly laid on. There would have been less worry had Wrightson and Jeremiah Fingleton been wholly amenable.

Fingleton, completely honest, was the chief worry. He knew that some plot was being hatched, wanted to warn McGinn and couldn't find him. He was at the hotel when Jolly talked to Bella Daventry, and he also decided to see the Toff.

Wrightson was watching him; and knew this.

Wrightson, already in bad with Rowe for selling the stolen gems, and heavily in debt, was terrified of what would happen if the Toff took a hand. Rowe had told him what to do if Fingleton looked like going to the police. So he had obeyed his orders, but his nerves had almost beaten him; in the end, they had.

Bella, already uneasy about the company's affairs, had seen the death of Jerry Fingleton. She had been worried about Rowe, her great benefactor, a man who had once meant more to her than her own father. She had wanted to find out from Wrightson if Rowe knew anything about the crimes. She had not bargained for the effect of Paul Wrightson's shattered nerves, the struggle and what had followed.

Rowe had telephoned her, soothed her fears, asked her to meet him at the Heybridge house. Even when Lemaitre had attacked her there, she had clung to belief in Rowe, believing him to be a victim rather than the rogue. She had wanted so desperately to believe in and to help the man who had meant so much to her.

Once the impersonation was started, Bella had to be kept away from "Connor McGinn", but not too obviously. Rory would not let her be hurt; the one good thing in Rory McGinn was his love for Bella. But although he knew that Rowe had planned her murder when at Heybridge, he hadn't the courage to strike back. His own future stood or fell by the success of the impersonation. He could hope at least for a share of the money and flight. To the last he swore that he had not planned his uncle's murder, or dreamt of killing Bella.

Rowe, meaning them both to die, had kept them alive only long enough to make sure of Rory's vital help. But the strain had told on

Rowe, too; after escaping from the police guard on the way to the airport, he had driven to the Isleworth house – not far away – to change into his Oval disguise. Rory had not known the house, but had the telephone number. He had telephoned, Rowe had told him to sit tight and wait, told him he needn't worry about the future, for both McGinn and Bella were to die.

"And Rory couldn't take it. He was bad, but not that bad," Grice said to Rollison, when the story had been pieced together. "He still lacked the guts to come and tell us, though. He'd actually betrayed Bella. She did telephone him from the call-box on Monday lunch-time. He told her to meet him at Putney, on Rowe's orders, and Rowe had men waiting to take her to the Isleworth house. She walked blindly into the trap because Rory had set it."

"Poor Bella," Rollison murmured gently.

"She's young, and she'll get over it," said Grice. "At least you were right about her. All right, all right," he added hastily, "you tumbled to the truth a long time before I did, too, and you also pointed at Rory. I surrender. But one of these days, Toff, you'll bite off much more than you can chew."

Rollison grinned.

"I mean it," Grice insisted. "You had a lot of luck with Black Norris. He still hasn't talked, but Rowe has. They had to find out if you'd seen McGinn, the real one—and incidentally," digressed Grice, smoothly, "you *had*. Only you, too."

"Back view," Rollison murmured, "and wearing the same clothes as the fake. But I promise you that I shall kick myself."

"Leave that to me. Where was I?" Grice rubbed the bridge of his nose. "Oh, Norris's first call on you. He wanted to find out whether you'd seen McGinn, and what you'd found at Wrightson's place. He didn't get the information, so you were still a danger. You were lured to Soho, where he was waiting to break your neck. After that, he was just killer-mad with you."

"But the police were on their guard," said Rollison solemnly.

"The police," declared Grice, "are always on their guard. You wouldn't care to know why Rowe went back to the Oval, would you?"

"Try me."

"He'd used the ground for years, to pass on stolen jewels and hot money," Grice said. "He sometimes did the ice-cream act, and so did others who worked with him. None of the officials ever took much notice of the regular Ovalites. It seemed a nice, secure spot. And they were all cricket fans, too. Bad types, these fans."

Rollison didn't bite.

"So the Oval was the obvious centre of operations," Grice went on. "Rowe had everything laid on to get the jewels, but nothing prepared to dispose of them. He knew the hunt would be up as soon as he vanished *en route* to the airport. He had to get the jewels distributed to different runners, and so turned into cash. In actual fact, as you know, he had them stuffed in the bottom of his ice cream box—his runners couldn't get through the crowd.

"Once he'd spread the risk, he would have gone to earth at Isleworth, collected from different fences, and got out of the country as soon as possible. If he'd had more time to plan, he would have had something different laid on, but he'd been at the Oval so often it seemed the safest place in the world. And," went on Grice, with a handsome smile, "so it would have been, if you hadn't been as crazy about cricket as the mob is itself."

"That's right," said Rollison. "We won, too, and I'll always be able to say I was there when it happened."

Rollison went to see Bella at the Miramar, that evening, where she was the guest of the real McGinn. She was taking it well. She had believed in Rowe and he had failed her dreadfully; she had fallen in love with Rory McGinn, a swindler and a cheat. He was under arrest for his part in the conspiracy; and would be severely punished. But it had become clear that he had known nothing of the murders, in advance, and he might even turn Queen's Evidence. He was young, and possibly had a future.

Now there was Bella, lying in bed, wearing the pale-pink angora bed-jacket which Rollison had sent round through Jolly. She had pecked at a meal, and had made-up a little when she had learned that Rollison was coming. She even forced a smile.

"All right," said Rollison, "all gone." He took her hands and kissed her gently. "Bygones are bygones, and Grice didn't do so badly after all. He swears that he was afraid that you'd meet trouble, that's really why he held you, and who am I to call him a liar? Anything you need to know?"

"No," she said. "Not really. I think I know everything. I don't think I'll ever be able to thank you."

"I'm not sure that you oughtn't to say that to Grice."

"Don't be absurd! There was that awful time at the bungalow, and—and—well, everything!"

Rollison laughed at her—

Before he left, she was laughing, too.

He went from her to the real McGinn, who said very little and that little to the point. He'd like to help that girl. He intended to stay for several weeks in England, and with her knowledge of jewels Bella could be invaluable. Would Rollison put a word in for him?

"She'll jump at the chance," Rollison assured him, "she desperately needs something to do."

He was quite sure that he was right.

Now and again, next day at the Oval, he thought of the girl and the real McGinn, who had started their business association that morning. He didn't think deeply. He watched Lindwall and Johnson fighting a losing battle as if they were bound to win. He saw England's runs come one by one, until the moment when the great crowd made its final roar and rose and surged upon the field to crowd round Mr. Compton and Mr. Edrich. He watched, as Bill Ebbutt and Bill's boys, at the front of the crowd, danced and cheered and capered as if the war of the worlds had been won.

Yet a year or so hence the battle would be joined again, in Australia; and in another English summer soon afterwards, Ebbutt and his men, probably Grice and perhaps even Jolly would all be there; and come crime as it may, so would the Toff.

JOHN CREASEY

GIDEON'S DAY

Gideon's day is a busy one. He balances family commitments with solving a series of seemingly unrelated crimes from which a plot nonetheless evolves and a mystery is solved.

One of the most senior officers within Scotland Yard, George Gideon's crime solving abilities are in the finest traditions of London's world famous police headquarters. His analytical brain and sense of fairness is respected by colleagues and villains alike.

'The finest of all Scotland Yard series' – New York Times.

GIDEON'S FIRE

Commander George Gideon of Scotland Yard has to deal successively with news of a mass murderer, a depraved maniac, and the deaths of a family in an arson attack on an old building south of the river. This leaves little time for the crisis developing at home ....

'Gideon of Scotland Yard emerges as one of the most real working detectives in modern fiction.... A sympathetic and believable professional policeman.' - New York Times

JOHN CREASEY

THE CREEPERS

"The prisoner's hand was thin and bony ... And in the centre of the palm was a pinkish mark. It was the shape of a wolf's head, mouth open, fangs showing.   Although it was what he had expected to see, Inspector West felt a twinge of repugnance a stab not unrelated to fear. It was the fifth time he had seen the mark of the wolf – the mark of Lobo."

A gang of cat burglars led by Lobo cause mayhem as they terrorize the city. They must be stopped, but with little in the way of evidence the police are baffled. Just how can Inspector West manage to do this in what is a race against time before more victims succumb?

"Here is an excellent novel of law enforcement officers, harried, discouraged and desperately fatigued, moving inexorably ahead under the pressure of knowledge that they must succeed to save human lives." - Cleveland Plain-Dealer

"Furiously exciting" - Chicago Tribune

"The action is fast, continuous and exciting" - San Francisco News

JOHN CREASEY

INTRODUCING THE TOFF

Whilst returning home from a cricket match at his father's country home, the Honourable Richard Rollison - alias The Toff - comes across an accident which proves to be a mystery. As he delves deeper into the matter with his usual perseverance and thoroughness , murder and suspense form the backdrop to a fast moving and exciting adventure.

'The Toff has been promoted to a place of honour among amateur detectives.' – The Times Literary Supplement

CASE AGAINST PAUL RAEBURN

Chief Inspector Roger West has been watching and waiting for over two years – he is determined to catch Paul Raeburn out. The millionaire racketeer may have made a mistake, following the killing of a small time crook.

Can the ace detective triumph over the evil Raeburn in what are very difficult circumstances? This cannot be assumed as not eveything, it would seem, is as simple as it first appears .....

'Creasey can drive a narrative along like nobody's business ... ingenious plot ... interesting background .' - The Sunday Times

15450077R00109

Printed in Poland
by Amazon Fulfillment
Poland Sp. z o.o., Wrocław